"Do I Know You?" Jennie Asked.

Did she? Had she ever really known him?

"Once..." Edward said, swallowing back every angry word he'd ever wanted to hurl at her, gentling his voice as he gentled his words.

She tightened her hand on his. "Before?"

"Yes," he said, knowing instinctively that she meant before whatever had brought her to Avalon.

Tears trembled on her lashes, and her soft lower lip quivered slightly. "Who are you?" she asked, grasping his arm. "Who am I?"

Edward covered her hand with his. How could he tell her she was his wife and that he desperately wanted her back?

* * *

"Ms. Moon writes with a spellbinding intensity that will keep you up till the wee hours of the morning until the last page is turned."
—Romantic Times

Dear Reader,

Can you believe that for the next three months we'll be celebrating the publication of the 1000th Silhouette Desire? That's quite a milestone! The festivities begin this month with six books by some of your longtime favorites and exciting new names in romance.

We'll continue into next month, May, with the actual publication of Book #1000—by Diana Palmer—and then we'll keep the fun going into June. There's just so much going on that I can't put it all into one letter. You'll just have to keep reading!

This month we have an absolutely terrific lineup, beginning with *Saddle Up*, a MAN OF THE MONTH by Mary Lynn Baxter. There's also *The Groom, I Presume?*— the latest in Annette Broadrick's DAUGHTERS OF TEXAS miniseries. *Father of the Brat* launches the new FROM HERE TO PATERNITY miniseries by Elizabeth Bevarly, and *Forgotten Vows* by Modean Moon is the first of three books about what happens on THE WEDDING NIGHT. Lass Small brings us her very own delightful sense of humor in *A Stranger in Texas*. And our DEBUT AUTHOR this month is Anne Eames with *Two Weddings and a Bride*.

And next month, as promised, Book #1000, a MAN OF THE MONTH, *Man of Ice* by Diana Palmer!

Lucia Macro,
Senior Editor

Please address questions and book requests to:
Silhouette Reader Service
U.S.: 3010 Walden Ave., P.O. Box 1325, Buffalo, NY 14269
Canadian: P.O. Box 609, Fort Erie, Ont. L2A 5X3

MODEAN MOON
MOON
FORGOTTEN VOWS

SILHOUETTE *Desire*
Published by Silhouette Books
America's Publisher of Contemporary Romance

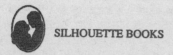 SILHOUETTE BOOKS

ISBN 0-373-05995-7

FORGOTTEN VOWS

Printed in U.S.A.

Books by Modean Moon

Silhouette Desire

The Giving #868
Interrupted Honeymoon #904
Forgotten Vows #995

MODEAN MOON

once believed she could do anything she wanted. Now she realizes there is not enough time in one life to do everything. As a result, she says her writing is a means of exploring paths not taken. Currently she works as a land-title researcher, determining land or mineral ownership for clients. Modean lives in Oklahoma on a hill overlooking a small town. She shares a restored Victorian farmhouse with a six-pound dog, a twelve-pound cat, and, reportedly, a resident ghost.

Dear Reader,

When asked to participate in the celebration of the one thousandth **Silhouette Desire**, I was honored. As a writer, I am relatively new to the line, but as a reader, I have been around since the beginning—as have many of you.

A thousand books? It didn't feel like nearly that many when I was anxiously waiting for the next month's selection because I had already read the current month's. Did it feel that way to you?

All I ever really wanted to do was tell stories. My favorite picture of me is at about age three, in the front yard with my dolls all lined up—a captive audience, indeed—to listen to the latest of my tales. Today I feel the same sense of wonder when I complete a story. And now, my readers can talk to me. When I receive a letter from Barbara or Martha or Lulu or you telling me how much you liked that story, or when you silently tell me by buying my book, I feel just like that delighted three-year-old in her short skirt and Mary Janes. Thank you, Desire, for making that possible.

As a writer, I feel constrained to be quiet and professional as I express my appreciation for the way my work has been received. But as a reader who still eagerly awaits the great selection of stories and characters and emotions available to us each month between these familiar red covers, what I most want to say is "Way to go, Desire! May there be many thousands more!"

Best wishes,

Modean Moon

Prologue

She would die.

That's what the doctors said when the woman was brought into the newly opened emergency trauma center of the small community hospital. But because they were doctors, and because this unconscious woman was the first true emergency to be brought into their shining new facility, they cleansed and patched and stitched so that when the moment of death came, which seemed imminent, she would at least be clean and whole. Then they called in the hospital chaplain.

The chaplain administered the sacrament of unction, then sat with the woman, who seemed little more than a child, mourning the waste of this young life and grieving for the pain this loss would cause her family, whoever they might be. But when she clung to life with a tenacity that amazed even him, he said a small prayer and contacted his cousin, vicar of the most affluent church in this well-to-do community for help.

It so happened that the lesson for the previous Sunday had been from the Gospel of Matthew. "... inasmuch as you have done it unto one of the least of these my brethren, ye have done it unto me," and the vicar had preached what he considered to be one of his finest sermons in almost fifty years of service, admonishing his flock to share their blessings as well as count them during the Thanksgiving season in order to prepare themselves for the coming season of Advent. Determined to discover the effectiveness of his sermon, the vicar called on one of the leaders of his congregation, the hospital administrator.

The hospital administrator was not willing to donate the use of an exorbitantly expensive bed in the intensive care unit to the still-unconscious, unidentified and probably uninsured woman, no matter how obviously fine her clothes had been prior to her injuries. But, with gentle prompting from the vicar, he recalled that a number of semiprivate rooms were not currently in use, and, since the staff and facilities were available, he consented, without grumbling about the cost, to letting her be installed in one such room.

She would die.

That's what the doctors said on the third day, when the infection in the woman's lungs became pneumonia and it was obvious that she had no resources left with which to fight the disease. But the vicar had been quite busy. Donations of flowers, money and nursing care flooded the hospital. The vicar stood back, smiling gently, pleased with his flock who had opened their hearts, or at least their pocketbooks, to this waif who had quite literally been dropped into their midst.

And still she clung to life.

Matilda Higgins was a retired registered nurse who had thought she was at long last through with all-night duty. Not having much of a pocketbook, though, and thinking of her own daughters and granddaughters, she had given what she could: her time—through the long hours after midnight.

Matilda sat in a comfortable chair in the hospital room, knitting by the light of a single, discreetly angled lamp, as she had for five nights, listening to the labored breathing of her patient. When the sounds of the young woman's breathing changed, Matilda put aside her knitting, walked to the side of the bed and studied the figure lying there with the observance that had carried her through years of successful nursing.

The patient moved restlessly, awkwardly, hampered by plaster casts and splints and tape and tubes. When she was first brought in, her dark brown hair had hung past her waist. It had been necessary to cut it close to her head in order to search out and remove tiny pellets of gravel and grit embedded in her scalp, to cleanse and treat the long gash. Now her small head, swathed in bandages, stirred on the pillows; her eyes opened for the first time since she'd been found.

She looked directly at Matilda without seeming to see her. Her mouth opened; a small tongue crept out to wet dry lips. "Renn?" she whispered, her voice cracked and rusty. *"Renn?"* And as strange as the word sounded to her, Matilda knew this must be someone's name.

Matilda wanted to take the woman's hand to calm the panic she heard in that lost voice, but that would have been awkward. Instead, she laid her hand on the woman's feverish forehead. "Renn's coming," she said in her most comforting tone, praying that this was in fact a name, and that she had repeated it correctly, praying that this was the right thing to say.

For a moment, an expression that could have been panic, or hope, lighted the unknown woman's eyes.

"What's your name?" Matilda murmured. "Tell me your name, love, so we can find Renn."

The woman in the bed closed her eyes, then opened them again, looking at, and also through, Matilda. With a little sigh, she sank against the pillow. ''I'm Jennie.''

One

An hour's hard drive north and east of El Paso, Edward William Renberg Carlton IV pulled his rented Jeep to the side of the road and stepped out, twisting and stretching to ease his cramped muscles and the knot of tension that had been tightening since the night before, when Simms had brought him the photograph.

His emotions had run the gamut the last six months—from fear to shock to anger. Now his heart and soul were desolate—as desolate as the harsh scrub-desert countryside around him, as desolate as they had been before a wisp of a girl had shown him color and shadings and laughter and, he'd thought, love. Desolate. Except for the knot of tension still tightening.

Edward reached into the Jeep and lifted the picture from its folder. She wasn't looking at the camera. In fact, she seemed to be unaware of it as she smiled wistfully at someone out of range of the camera's eye. She'd cut her magnificent hair. Now only a short cap of curls framed her delicate face. She'd shed weight she didn't need to lose, honed down, and lost the last vestiges of youthful softness.

"Damn it!" he muttered, forcing his fist to relax before he crushed the photograph. "Why?"

But neither the prairie dogs, the coyotes, the hawks nor the scruffy cactus answered him.

He stopped again much later, just outside the town of Avalon, his destination. A mile after leaving the highway, on a curve overlooking the naturally terraced mountainside, he pulled to the verge and looked through a break in the trees—towering pines, majestic oak, hickories and walnuts—at a town that seemed out of someone's fantasy. He'd expected rural Southwest, perhaps even mountainous West, not a turn-of-the-century village. Not abundant, manicured and carefully planted and tended green.

He shook his head once, as though to clear it, and heard a bell, a church bell, tolling the hour. From where he'd stopped, he could see at least three churches—white frame, red brick, and one gray stone.

Leave it to Jennie to find a place like this. He felt his pain rising to choke him and fought it the only way he knew how, with his anger. Damn it! *Damn her!* Her whole life had been an illusion. Why should her hiding place be any different? And damn him for giving her the power to hurt him.

If he'd gone to the apartment he kept in the city last night instead of lingering at the office, Simms wouldn't have found him to show him the picture that had ripped open wounds he'd convinced himself had begun to heal. If Madeline, his administrative assistant, had had her way, if he hadn't heard her arguing in his outer office, Simms wouldn't have been allowed in to show him the picture. Madeline was only trying to protect him, as she had for years. She couldn't understand why he had to know, had to confront, had to ask, "Why?"

The eight-by-ten black-and-white photo and accompanying text had been sent to Simms, the city editor of San Francisco's largest newspaper, with a polite inquiry as to whether it would rate a small feature, and, if not, would Mr. Simms please refer the material to the advertising department for a paid ad. The letter was signed by Wilbur Winthrop, vicar of St. Alban's Church, Avalon, New Mexico, and said simply, "Do you know this woman?" The vicar had no way of knowing the Carlton family had owned that newspaper for four generations. Or had he?

Edward had taken the picture from Madeline and the letter from Simms before Madeline had a chance to see it. He'd left his office, taking Simms with him long enough to swear him to secrecy about the photo and the contact's name and address, then left the building. Later, after Madeline had left no fewer than five messages on his answering machine, and had come to his apartment but had not gotten past the new security guard, he'd left that building, too. And finally, he'd left the city.

There was a small airport just outside of Avalon. Edward had noticed that while readying to leave. But he'd flown his executive jet into El Paso instead, because he hadn't been sure of the availability of a rental car, hadn't been sure he wanted to announce his presence in Avalon so blatantly and hadn't been sure he wanted anyone in his offices to know where he'd gone or the folly that had brought him here. In the anonymous Jeep, he could look over the situation and leave, if he wanted, without anyone's—without Jennie's—ever knowing he'd been here; leave—without seeing her.

If she's here.

For the first time since seeing the photograph, his mind began to clear. Why would the vicar place an ad like that if she were still here? Had she used the vicar, too? The woman he'd thought he'd known wouldn't have—couldn't have. But then, the woman he'd thought he'd known wouldn't have disappeared with a hundred thousand dollars' worth of bonds from his safe and after finding them nonnegotiable, she wouldn't have ripped the stones from the rings he'd given her, returning to him only the mangled settings.

The gray stone church was St. Alban's. Ivy grew up the wall overlooking a well-tended cemetery on the church grounds. New plantings of spring flowers bordered the sidewalks leading to the red double doors of the graceful building. The vicarage sat to one side and slightly back from the road. Like the church, the cottage was a small stone structure that needed only a thatched roof to complete the fairy-tale setting.

Edward stood on the front steps, folder in hand, and sounded the door knocker before he had time to question again the wisdom of his being there. The door opened quickly, and he found himself facing a pleasant-looking older woman.

"Good afternoon," she said, smiling. "May I help you?" Her voice was pleasant, too, well modulated, as gracious as her surroundings, and bearing a faint trace of an English accent. In spite of the gravity of the situation, Edward felt an answering smile begging to be set free, and wondered, not for the first time since seeing the village, if magically, he had been transported to some alternate reality.

"I'd like to speak with Reverend Winthrop, please," he said.

Not by a flicker of a lash did the woman reveal any curiosity. "Certainly," she said, opening the door wider and stepping back. "Won't you come in? My husband is in his study. If you'll wait in the front parlor—" she gestured to a room opening off the foyer "—I'll tell him you're here."

She hadn't even asked his name, he mused as he walked into the parlor. But perhaps as a vicar's wife, she was accustomed to strange men knocking on her door, asking for her husband.

Or she already knew who he was.

Glancing about the room, his eye fell upon the painting. He felt as though someone had just slammed a two-by-four across his midsection. The pain was that instantaneous, that severe, when he saw the framed watercolor hanging over the mantel. He didn't have to look at the artist's signature; he recognized the work—a misty, otherworldly representation of the harbor during a festival of antique sailing vessels.

"That's truly a remarkable painting, isn't it?" a man asked from behind him. Edward used the excuse of studying the painting to calm his features and his emotions.

"My daughter sent that to me for Christmas," the man continued. "I've asked her to find me more by this artist—Allison Long—but the cost of her work has skyrocketed. Oh, well. I suppose it is inevitable with talent like that. I should be grateful for the one I have."

Was this man for real?

Edward schooled his features and turned slowly. The man across the room appeared guileless and innocent and a fitting partner for the woman who had admitted Edward to the house.

"I'm familiar with—with Ms. Long's work," Edward said softly, waiting.

The older man smiled. "Then we've both been blessed." Then, slightly more formally, he extended his hand. "I'm Wilbur Winthrop. How may I be of assistance, Mr...."

"Carlton," Edward told him, looking for any sign of recognition or hesitation in the vicar's eyes and finding none. "Edward Carlton."

"Please," Winthrop said, gesturing toward a chintz-covered easy chair. "Sit down, Mr. Carlton. You seem . . . agitated. Would you care for some tea?"

"No, I—" *Was he that easy to read?* Edward sat in the proffered chair but refused to sink into its depths. He glanced at the folder in his hand, opened it and held the picture toward the vicar. "I'm here because of this."

"Ah, Jennie," Winthrop said. "Oh, my, that was fast. It doesn't seem possible there has been enough time for it to appear in the paper and bring you here."

That was neatly done, Edward recognized. Instead of being defensive, or volunteering information, the wily old minister was questioning *him*.

"The city editor knew of my interest," Edward told him. A new thought lodged. "Did you send this to several papers or only—only the one?"

"Just the one, for a beginning," Winthrop told him, taking a matching chair facing Edward and leaning forward. "And your interest in her . . . ?"

"Why?"

Winthrop blinked. "Why?"

"Why just the one paper?"

"Oh, because of its circulation. And because of her clothes. Marianna Richards recognized the one label we found as being from an exclusive San Francisco shop. *And your interest in her?*" he asked again.

Edward sighed. "What did she do? And how long has she been gone?"

"*Do? Jennie?* What makes you think Jennie did anything? And Mr. Carlton—" his voice lowered, firmed "—I really must insist you answer my question. What is your interest in our Jennie?"

Our Jennie? Edward took a deep, sustaining breath. "She didn't mention me?"

The vicar shook his head slowly. "She mentioned only one person, if indeed she did mention anyone. Matilda was with her that night and isn't sure she heard properly. It was a strange name, if a name at all."

Edward studied the man across from him. He didn't appear to be a victim, didn't appear to be a conspirator. And, God knew, Edward had to trust someone. "I last saw her on the seventeenth of November."

Winthrop nodded. "She came to us the week before Thanksgiving."

"Less than—less than eight hours after our wedding."

"Oh, my. Oh, my. Oh, dear," the vicar said.

"When did she leave?" Edward asked, and questions welled up inside of him, spilling into the peace of the room. "How long was she here? What did she do that you found it necessary to run *this*?" He looked at the folder in his hand. "Did she know about it?"

He felt a hand on his shoulder and looked up into the compassionate eyes of Wilbur Winthrop, who now stood before him.

"Mr. Carlton..." The vicar shook his head and crossed the room to a small cabinet, took out a glass and bottle and poured a drink, which he brought to Edward. He took Edward's free hand and wrapped it around the squat, heavy crystal glass. "Medicinal," he said in the same low, firm voice he had used in questioning Edward. "You really should drink it."

Edward considered the vicar's words and nodded. Winthrop had poured only an ounce or so of liquid into the glass. Edward drank it in two swallows, shuddered once and returned the glass to the minister. Winthrop patted his shoulder once again, placed the glass on a nearby table and resumed his place in the chair facing Edward. Leaning forward, elbows on his knees, he hesitated briefly as if carefully considering his words before speaking.

"Jennie came to us under extremely unusual circumstances, Mr. Carlton. And by being the warm, loving, gentle woman she is, she has touched all of us in this community."

Winthrop's smile was both self-deprecating and a little wry. "In case you didn't notice, Avalon is . . . well, unique. And those of us who live here—who have lived here for generations—have become complacent and, to put it bluntly, more than a little smug about our obviously superior place in the world."

Pausing briefly, the vicar continued. "Jennie's needs—"

"What?"

Winthrop shook his head. "In good time, Mr. Carlton. You of all persons must know how special she is. Jennie's needs jarred our self-created pedestals, forced us to look at ourselves and to reach into ourselves to give help to someone other than us or our immediate own. To give—because Jennie is who she is, because she responded to our care and caring with such openness and innocence—to give *love* to someone other than us or our immediate own."

Edward again felt questions building inside of him. This woman the vicar described was the woman he'd thought he'd known, not the woman who'd left him. He felt his features hardening. What the hell was going on? He lifted the folder, now caught in a death grip.

"If she's so open and honest and loving, then why—why did you find it necessary to do this?"

Winthrop reached over and peeled Edward's fingers from the folder, which he dropped to the floor beside the chair.

"I'm sure our sheriff will want to ask you some questions, Mr. Carlton—"

"What—"

"Jennie was injured when she came to us."

Edward felt himself trying to jerk to his feet, but Winthrop had hold of his hands, patting them as consolingly as he had earlier patted Edward's shoulder. "I didn't tell Jennie of my plans to contact various newspapers because I didn't want to agitate her—or raise any false hope."

"She's still here, then?"

Winthrop nodded.

"Then why was the picture necessary? Why didn't you just *ask* this open, honest, innocent?"

Winthrop looked at him through ageless, knowing eyes. "There is so much pain in you. What could have caused this?"

"Ask her."

"I wish I could, Mr. Carlton. I pray daily for that option." He raised one hand, either in supplication or to stop Edward's continued attempts to stand. "I told you that Jennie was injured. It was rather more than a minor accident. We almost lost her. Even some of her doctors lost heart, at least for a while. I don't ask her because she doesn't know, Mr. Carlton. When she regained consciousness, Jennie had no memory of anything that had gone before."

The concrete bench sat in a shaded arbor in the vicarage garden and was slightly cool, but the May sunshine, dappled through the leaves, and the gentle breeze were caressingly warm. Jennie raised her face to both sun and wind and laughed softly in delight.

"There, love," Matilda said from her protective stance beside her. "Didn't I promise you would enjoy this?"

"That you did, Matilda."

"Now, drink your tea."

Jennie grimaced but spoke with mellow good nature. "You're beginning to sound like a nanny again, Mrs. Higgins."

"Oops. Sorry."

But Jennie could tell that the woman wasn't sorry at all. She smiled in the general direction of her mother hen, took a sip from her cup, set it on the bench beside her and reached for Matilda's hand. "Now, the guided tour you promised me. Please."

"Where shall we start? The herb garden? The perennial garden? There is some spring color there. Or the maze?"

Jennie breathed deeply, fighting the sense of frustration and loss that bombarded her, fighting the tears that welled in her eyes. "Let's start with something simple," she suggested, hating the quaver she heard in her voice, "something I'm at least a little familiar with." She found a bright smile for Matilda—the woman deserved no less. "Let's start with—"

"Matilda? Mrs. Higgins?" Reverend Winthrop called from the house.

Matilda put a comforting hand on Jennie's shoulder. "Would you like to wait here? I'll just hurry and see what he wants and be right back."

Jennie smiled and nodded. "Of course. I'm enjoying being out here. Take your time."

She'd finished her tea, and Matilda still hadn't returned. The bench was getting cooler. And the ray of sun had moved so that it no longer lay warm on her face. Jennie squirmed on the bench, easing tight muscles and trying to ignore the growing sensation of someone, or something, watching her. Maybe she could walk a short distance by herself. The paths were well defined; she'd learned that already. And the garden was walled—she'd learned that, too—so there was no way she could get lost.

The fine hairs on her nape prickled; her arms responded to the caress of unseen eyes. She twisted on the bench to face the direction from which those sensations seemed to come. "Is anyone there?" she whispered.

She shook her head, answering her own question. "Of course not." Of course there wasn't anyone there. The birds were still chirping merrily. She was just being . . . fanciful. She supposed it was the newness of being alone in the garden. She really ought to take advantage of this opportunity for independence. Her keepers were loving but much too protective. Surely she had some skills. But how was she ever going to discover them unless she explored?

For a moment, fear tightened her throat and raced her heart. For a moment, her hands clenched on the edge of the bench. She could do this! She *could*. Then she became aware again of the sensation of unseen eyes watching her. Panic welled up within her, unexpected and unexplainable. Giving a little cry, Jennie rose from the bench and stumbled along the garden walk.

Edward stood in the shade of an ancient oak tree watching the woman on the bench. She was lovely—self-contained, beautiful. His wife. He felt pain twisting inside him again, as demanding and unwelcome as the desire that tightened and readied his body as he let his wayward eyes caress her.

For a few minutes after the older woman left her, Jennie had sat calmly, to all appearances enjoying her solitude. And Jennie in repose was truly beautiful—truly a beautiful sight in any attitude, he corrected. He'd always been aware of that, but the past six months had refined her beauty. He mourned the loss of her hair, but without the weight of its length, it curled softly—a dark chestnut cap to frame her finely drawn features and emphasize dark brown eyes that had always seemed to be alight with the joy of discovery.

A wide-brimmed, floppy hat with ribbon streamers lay on the bench beside Jennie, and she was wearing a softly floral-patterned, flowing dress. Edward felt the pressure of his lips drawn against his teeth. *How appropriate, Jennie,* he thought. *And how much in character for your setting.*

Did she really not remember the past? Edward doubted that, just as he doubted she would thank the minister for his well-intentioned interference with her plans for a haven.

He couldn't fault Reverend Winthrop for his innocence, for being taken in by Jennie's act. Hell! He'd been deceived, too. And he was experienced in facing the dark side of his fellow creatures. Before Jennie, many had tried; the Carlton money, the Carlton power were too tempting for a greedy person to pass by without at least attempting to gain some. He'd learned that in a harsh and well-remembered school. But until Jennie, no one had succeeded in getting past the defenses he had so painstakingly constructed.

He clenched his hands into fists. *Damn it, Jennie! Why? I wanted to give you the world. I wanted to give you my heart.*

And that, of course, answered his question. The world, Jennie would have taken. It was Edward she didn't want. And although that knowledge still had the power to hurt, it had no power to surprise him. He had always wondered how the laughing, delightful, loving woman he'd thought he'd known could love *him,* reserved, incapable of voicing even the simplest terms of affection or letting himself believe that love truly existed—unless what she felt for him was really only pity.

Well, he'd been wrong. About himself. About her. Love existed. It had trapped him in a hell from which he might never escape. And pity hadn't controlled Jennie's actions toward him. Greed had. Why hadn't he listened to Madeline from the beginning? Madeline was more than a trusted employee, she was the closest thing to a friend he had allowed himself in years.

As though the turbulence of his thoughts had somehow called out to her, the woman on the bench twisted slightly, raised a hand to the back of her neck and appeared to be listening. Edward leaned back against the tree, deeper in the shadows. He would announce himself soon—Winthrop had granted him only a few minutes alone with her—but not yet. He felt strangely debilitated, unsure of himself and of his ability to confront this woman who had betrayed his deepest trust.

Not yet.

Again, Jennie fidgeted on the bench, but this time she turned, too, until she faced him. Looking almost directly at the spot where he stood beneath the tree, she whispered, "Is anyone there?" Then her eyes darkened. She shook her head. "Of course not," she said in the same tense whisper. She seemed to listen for a moment longer, her hands clenched on the edge of the bench. Then, with a soft cry that could have been a moan or a plea, she rose from the bench like a startled fawn unused to its new legs, and stumbled away from him, along the brick walk.

Edward's eyebrows drew together in a stunned frown. Jennie was a graceful woman, as light, as ethereal on her feet as a moonbeam. Why then this halting, awkward gait?

He saw the raised bricks of the path where an ancient root had tunneled beneath and lifted them; Jennie apparently did not. With a startled cry, she fell, tumbling from the path and into a bed of some green ground-cover. Edward started toward her, but something about her actions slowed his steps.

Her eyes filled with tears. "Damn," she moaned, flailing at the ground with tiny balled fists. "Damn! Damn! *Damn!*"

She took a deep, shuddering breath and knelt there in the plants for a moment, as still as death, then began patting the earth in front of her, as though looking for something. When her hands encountered the brick walk, she crawled forward until she touched the elevated bricks. She patted them three or four times as though validating their existence or confirming their blame for her fall.

She dragged herself to her feet and shuffled carefully onto the path, then stood very still.

And Edward stood equally still, transfixed by the actions of this woman he had once called a wood sprite.

Jennie took one careful step, then stopped. She turned and reached in front of her, groping at space as she took another step.

Edward saw her eyes, troubled, filled with frustration. Tears quivered on her lashes. She bit at her lower lip, and her eyes darkened, the frustration shifting, changing to—to panic?

"Is anyone there?" she whispered again, her hands extended, palms out. "Please. I can feel you here. Please. Please say something."

And the truth slammed into Edward with the force of the worst pain he had ever felt—the pain of knowing she was truly gone, that after enticing, inviting and winning his love, she had left him.

The truth. Oh, God. Edward bit back the involuntary cry that lodged near his heart.

Jennie Carlton, his wife—Allison Jennifer Long Carlton—the artist whose work Wilbur Winthrop declared had blessed both their lives—Jennie was blind.

Two

She was broken, and even she didn't know how badly.

In the long hours of the previous night, Edward had plotted what he would do today. He'd promised himself he would see Jennie, show his contempt for her and her larcenous heart, give in to Madeline's prudent suggestions to file for divorce and then—oh, God—and then find some way to take his much-needed revenge.

But now that he had seen her, Edward knew he could do none of the rest.

Revenge? He remembered Jennie's eyes—laughing, glowing with what he'd thought was love, lost in contemplation of the work on her latest canvas. He thought of the stacks of completed work that had filled her studio, of the color and beauty with which she had always surrounded herself, and another small piece of him died. He felt that piece shift and tear. Curious, he thought numbly. He had thought himself past grief.

"Please," Jennie whispered again.

Edward took a deep breath. Revenge? This was beyond anything his fertile mind would have—could have come up with.

"Don't be alarmed," he said softly, walking to her side. He reached for her. "Here I am. Take my hand."

Jennie closed her eyes briefly as she slid her hand into his much larger one and tilted her head to look up toward him, just as she had countless times in the past. Edward watched the panic fade from her beautiful eyes. For a moment, forgetting, Edward expected recognition to flood them. For a moment, he expected her to smile, to whisper his name with that breathless catch of anticipation that had always beguiled him.

Instead, he saw a curious blankness in the depths of her eyes, a subtle, almost unnoticeable lack of focus, and then, finally, faint confusion.

"Do I know you?" Jennie asked.

Did she? Had she ever really known him? "Once," he said, swallowing back every angry word he'd ever wanted to hurl at her, gentling his voice as he gentled his words.

She tightened her hand in his and reached with her other hand to grip his arm. "Before?"

"Yes," he said, knowing instinctively that she meant before whatever had brought her to Avalon. "Before."

Tears trembled once again on her lashes, and her soft lower lip quivered slightly before she covered it with one fragile hand and closed her eyes against an emotion so strong, Edward felt it vibrate through her, and because of their joined hands, through him.

"Oh, thank God," she said. "I thought—I was afraid no one would look for me."

Edward heard a world of fear and loneliness in her words, far more than seemed possible in the pleasant surroundings of the vicarage garden.

"Who are you?" Jennie asked him, once again grasping his arm. "Who am I?"

Edward covered her hand with his, marveling as always at the contrast between her soft, fair, almost translucent skin and his rougher, darker, almost swarthy coloring. He didn't know which of them was trembling; it didn't seem to matter. What mattered was the emotion that gathered in his throat, making speech all but impossible. What mattered was this fragile, delicate woman who was looking up at him with such hope. How could he tell her who she was and what she had done? How could he even believe it himself?

Why had Jennie left him? Not for money. He'd bet his life on that. Now. How—why—had he ever thought her capable of that?

His arms ached with his need to pull her close, to hold her against his heart, to fill his senses with her light perfume, to take the comfort her arms, to feel the passion her sweet body had always brought him. Instead, he restrained himself, limiting himself to smoothing his hand over hers one more time before taking a step away, still holding her hand. A lifeline, he thought, looking at their entwined fingers. But for her? Or for himself?

"I think—" Remarkable. His voice almost worked. But what could he tell her? "I think before either of us says much more, we need to talk with Reverend Winthrop."

A second man was waiting in the parlor with Reverend Winthrop. He studied Edward critically and narrowed his eyes when he saw what Edward only now noticed: Jennie's scraped knees and the small tear in her skirt. At about six foot two, the man stood eye to eye with Edward, although he probably carried a few more well-muscled pounds than Edward. He had the look of a battered warrior, in his eyes and in the lines of his face. Edward had no doubt that somewhere on his person, this man carried a badge of some sort—a fact that was quickly confirmed.

"Good afternoon, Miss Jennie," he said in a gravelly voice that carried the remnants of a soft southern drawl.

Jennie smiled toward him. "Good afternoon, Sheriff Lambert. Isn't it wonderful? This man knows me."

"Might be, Miss Jennie. Might be. You hurt yourself?"

Jennie grimaced and sighed. "Am I a mess? I fell. It was stupid, I know. To fall, I mean. I was trying to walk in the garden alone. But, Sheriff Lambert, this man knows who I am. He said he wouldn't tell me until we came back to the house. Ask him. Please ask him."

Lambert put both his hands on Jennie's shoulders, with the familiarity of someone who had done so many times before, and Edward forced himself to deny the tension that tightened in him.

"I will, Miss Jennie. But now I want you to go upstairs with Mrs. Higgins and take care of your lovely knees."

Jennie straightened her small shoulders, and Edward recognized the defiant lift of her chin. "Sheriff Lambert," she said in the same gentle voice Edward had once heard her use on a gallery owner who had made the mistake of thinking he could lie to her about sales of her work, "in spite of appearances and circumstances, I am a mature adult. I will not be sent to my room like a child."

"No, Miss Jennie, and I wouldn't do that to you, either. But I'm going to talk to this man and find out who he is before I let him try to tell me who you are. When I'm satisfied, we'll all talk together. And that's a promise. Until then, you just don't go getting your emotions in a lather.

"You've been hurt enough, and none of us," he continued, giving her shoulders a little shake, "none of us is going to let you be hurt again. Understand?"

After Jennie and a woman introduced as Mrs. Higgins left the parlor, Edward walked to the fireplace and looked again at the framed watercolor. His ship, the *Lady B,* named by his father years earlier, created the visual focus for the painting. Even at rest, bare-masted, with no sign of

a crew, she seemed to dance in the water, to shimmer across
the misty canvas.

He bowed his head in his hand. What now? How had
Jennie come to Avalon? Why had she come to Avalon?
And how had she been hurt? He straightened his shoulders, drawing his strength around him, and turned. Wilbur Winthrop was still standing near the door to the
hallway. Edward pierced him with an accusing glare.

"You didn't tell me she was blind."

The two other men exchanged a long, measuring look,
but it was Lambert who spoke. "Well, now, that answers
one question, but it sure does raise up a host of others."

"I'll need to use your telephone," Edward told the minister. "I have to call my assistant, arrange to have my plane
flown here, put a—a what?—a neurologist? on standby,
have someone get my apartment ready for Jennie—"

"I don't think so."

The quiet determination in Lambert's voice put an
abrupt end to Edward's disjointed planning.

"You don't think so? Sheriff, I have every right to take
my wife home." Edward heard the words spilling from his
mouth.

Where had those words come from? He had fully in-
tended to leave her to her own devices, with her greed to
keep her company. *Greed? Jennie?*

He felt a hand on his arm and dimly realized Winthrop
had led him across the room, was pushing him down into
the chintz-covered chair, was once again wrapping his fingers around a squat, heavy glass. "Drink," Winthrop insisted. "You look like the walking wounded."

Edward did as he was told. He laid his head back against
the chair and drew deep, even breaths, at first barely aware
of what he was doing, then gradually recognizing what was
happening to him. He began fighting the shock, fighting
the fear and anger that had waited just below his con-

sciousness to claim him. Gradually, he summoned the strength of will that had sustained him over the years.

He couldn't come apart now; he hadn't since his parents' deaths, and he'd been only ten at the time. He was an adult now, a grown man who could face any problem.

He became aware of the force with which he grasped the chair's arms, of the silence in the room broken only by the ticking of a clock, of his own breathing. He became aware of Lambert watching him. Slowly, he released his grip on the chair, eased his breathing and met Sheriff Lambert's steady gaze. Instead of the derision or pity he expected to find in the sheriff's eyes, Edward found a grudging respect, as well as a wariness he felt sure this battle-weary warrior showed everyone.

"I have some questions for you, Mr. Carlton," Lambert said, taking a small notebook from his suit coat and making no reference to what had just passed. "Let's start with Jennie's full name."

"Allison Jennifer Carlton," Edward told him in the same dispassionate tone of voice the sheriff used. Then, realizing Jennie had claimed the name Carlton for only a few hours before she disappeared, he added, a little too loudly in the waiting silence of the room. "Long. Her maiden name was Long."

He saw Winthrop's head jerk up, saw the horrified questioning glance the minister shot at the watercolor he so prized.

"Yes," Edward told him, without waiting for the man to ask. "Yes," he said, sighing, expelling a little of his own pain. "Jennie is *that* Allison Long."

Jennie leaned back in the chaise longue in her room, her knees faintly smarting from the antiseptic Matilda had applied, her ego faintly smarting from being sent to her room.

Her life was being discussed downstairs. She had a right to be there. She had a right to have a voice in any decision made.

She smiled ruefully. Sheriff Lambert was probably right to exclude her. Apparently, she hadn't done such a bang-up job of running her own life until now.

Her finger ached. Absently, she rubbed it, as she found herself doing often when she tried to put order to the puzzle of her life. The doctors told her they could fix it—a simple surgical procedure—rebreak the bone, set it properly. Jennie shivered. She'd had enough pain to last a lifetime. Too much pain, she acknowledged, remembering how it had been when she first woke up in the Avalon hospital.

She closed her eyes, and the field behind her closed lids grew dark. It wasn't always dark; it was—it was more like walking into a dense fog just after twilight. Interesting, she thought. A new analogy. Before, she had compared her lack of sight to trying to look through layer upon layer of vaporous gray scarves.

When she slept, she had vision: color—vibrating, shimmering color—if not always shape. And sometimes her dreams were peopled. One person appeared repeatedly—a tall, stern man. In her dreams, she teased him, sensing it might somehow be similar to baiting a tiger. And although she never clearly saw his face, on rare occasions she found her efforts rewarded by a rusty, little-used smile.

Was he the one who had come for her?

She had been so afraid—When? Jennie couldn't consciously remember feeling the soul-shriveling depth of fear she now knew had once gripped her. When?

"Here you go, love," Matilda said as she entered the room. "Blackberry tea and some of Mrs. Winthrop's wonderful chicken salad."

Jennie looked up, not distracted by Matilda's loving offering. The man who had come for her was tall. Was he...dark? Was he...stern?

"Matilda," Jennie asked. "The man who—the man downstairs—what does he look like?"

"Ah, Jennie, Jennie," the older woman said softly, sitting beside her on the chaise and placing the tray across Jennie's lap. "I suppose he's a fine-looking man, healthy, strong of will and body, but, child, he doesn't look like he's ever in his life smiled."

Sheriff Lucas Lambert's office was in keeping with the affluence of the town: state-of-the-art computers and communications equipment shared spacious, carpeted quarters with high-tech filing and retrieval systems, well-designed furniture and cubicle dividers and professionally uniformed employees.

The office was distinctly out of keeping with the rugged, world-weary man who seated himself behind his oversize mahogany desk and glanced quickly through a file a deputy had handed him as he and Edward had entered the building.

Lambert tossed the folder onto his desk, glanced at it, glanced at Edward, opened a desk drawer and brought out a much fatter folder and placed it beside the first one. He took the pen and small notebook from his jacket and aligned them with the folders. He picked up the pen, rolling it between his fingers as he studied Edward. Then, apparently reaching a decision, he dropped the pen to the desktop. "Your identity checks out."

Seated in a chair in front of the desk, Edward only nodded. He was unaccustomed to being doubted, surprised there had ever been any question of his truthfulness.

"You didn't report your wife missing."

"There didn't seem much point in reporting anything," Edward said tightly. "I had a—a farewell note from her telling me how much better her life would be without me in it."

"Didn't you find it a little strange that your wife of—what?—eight hours or so just up and took off?"

"Hell, yes, I found it strange," Edward said with quiet fury. "As strange as the fact that our airline reservations for our trip to Hawaii had unexplainably been rescheduled for a later flight, as strange as the fact that my private office was burglarized that afternoon requiring me to go down there. As strange as the fact that when I returned to my home, my brand-new wife, one hundred thousand dollars' worth of bonds and several other reasonably valuable items were missing. As strange as the fact that when I went to Jennie's studio, trying to make sense of what had happened, I found it stripped of any sign of her, including all of her unsold work.

"Yes, Lambert. I found it damned strange. But I had a note from her. A note, damn it man, that stripped me as bare as that studio. A note taunting me with the wonderful new life she was going to lead once she broke free from me."

Lambert leaned back in his chair, once again sliding his pen through his fingers, once again seeming to come to a decision. He stood and nudged the fatter of the two folders across the desk toward Edward. "Take a look at this while I change clothes. Then we'll both go take a look at the place where your new bride spent two, maybe three days of that wonderful new life."

Edward was feeling sick, physically ill, when Lambert returned to the office wearing jeans and climbing boots and carrying a lightweight jacket. He dropped another pair of boots at Edward's feet.

"You'll need these," Lambert said. "I think they'll fit you."

Edward closed the file, but he couldn't close away the memory of the police photographs or the medical reports. He couldn't close away the rage that he felt growing inside him—the need to hit—to hurt. He held his hand flat on the cover of the folder as if by doing so he could hold all its horrible contents away from him, away from Jennie. God, no wonder she didn't remember. Thank God she didn't remember.

"What did this to her?"

Lambert took the folder from him and put it back in the desk drawer before he answered. "For a while, I entertained the thought that maybe you did this to her."

They took the sheriff's Land Rover. They'd driven for over an hour, most of it on narrow dirt roads, the last fifteen or twenty minutes uphill on a rutted, hole-pocked narrow trail. They'd long before left the green surrounding Avalon and had entered what Edward had always thought typical of eastern New Mexico—harsh, rocky land, barren except for scattered cactus, which now, but only for a few short days, blazed with color, outcroppings of rock, the badlands of hundreds of B-grade western movies, and mountains—harsh and unforgiving.

Lambert eased his vehicle across a boulder-strewn dry gully, left the track and pulled to a stop at the edge of the precipice that overlooked the dry bed of some ancient ocean.

"Watch your step," Lambert told him and felt his way over the edge and onto a barely visible animal trail. With only one quick glance toward the valley floor, Edward followed, feeling rocks sliding beneath his sturdy boots.

Finally, they reached an outcropping of rock that formed a narrow ledge and an overhang that created a sort of cave. The animal trail continued downward, but Lambert stopped.

"There are two ways to get here," Lambert told him. "Up from the valley floor, or down from the ridge." He pointed to a shallow depression beneath the overhang.

"Two high-school boys cutting class and out exploring for outlaw gold found Jennie there.

"We don't know when she lost her sight, but even sighted, there's no way she got here by herself. She either fell or was pushed from about where we parked."

In the last few hours, Edward had been hit with almost more than he could stand. For his sanity, for Jennie's sake, he had to emotionally separate Jennie from this anonymous broken woman who had been discarded on a New Mexico mountainside. He had to get his protective armor in place, had to stop acting like a terrified ten-year-old. Never again, he'd promised himself years ago, would he give in to the nameless, numbing horror he had once experienced. And he hadn't. Until now. But not until Jennie had he let himself be vulnerable again.

"You're sure she didn't come here for some reason?"

"What reason?" Lambert asked. "And yes, I'm sure. She couldn't have walked it. The trail down from the top is a cakewalk compared to the one up from the valley floor. And we found no vehicle.

"You last saw her on the seventeenth of November," Lambert asked abruptly. "What was she wearing?"

What was she wearing? For a moment, the memory swirled through Edward's mind.

He pulled the sheet over Jennie's bare shoulder and smoothed the dark hair away from her cheek, placing a kiss that was much more chaste than anything he felt at that moment on the tender skin he had just exposed.

"God, I hate to leave you," he told her, tracing his finger over her cheek, outlining lips that only a short while before had driven him nearly crazy with her untutored passion.

"And I hate for you to leave, but you know Madeline wouldn't have called unless it was important," she said.

"Are you all right?" he asked her. "Really all right? I didn't hurt you?"

She grinned at him then. "One of my deepest, darkest secrets is this hidden desire I've had to be ravished by a loving madman. Edward?" She sat up in the bed, letting the sheet fall away from her as she captured his face in her small hands.

"Edward, I'm teasing you. Of course you didn't hurt me. You'd never do that."

"She was—she was dressing for dinner," he said, forcing himself back to the present. "We were going to go out to eat when I returned . . . before we caught our flight." Edward threw off his memories. "Could she have parked somewhere else and walked in?"

Lambert shook his head. "She was wearing a white silk dress, silk lingerie. No jewelry. No hose. No shoes. The boys found her on the twenty-first."

"So she had four days to get here." Edward focused his thoughts on those days rather than on the way Jennie had looked in the photos. "Four days to—to do what?"

Again Lambert shook his head. "I think she was here at least as early as the nineteenth."

"Why?"

"It rained on the nineteenth. Her clothes were . . . muddy."

"Who?" Edward shouted. It was either shout or scream. He looked at the ridge above him. "What kind of animal would do this?"

"I don't know," Lambert told him. He studied Edward carefully. "And until I find out, Jennie's a ward of the court. I'm her guardian. Until we find whoever did this, I'm not letting you take her out of my jurisdiction."

Edward met Lambert's appraisal with one of his own. "I won't try to," he admitted. "It doesn't seem I've done too good a job of protecting her. I appreciate all the help I can get. I do want to bring some of my people here, make arrangements to stay as long as necessary. I'm not leaving Jennie."

Lambert nodded his agreement. "I've got some ideas of my own now that we know who she is, but do you have any suggestions as to how we find the bastard who did this?"

Edward looked over the valley floor. He wasn't ready, or able, yet, even to consider that Jennie had been taken from him, that she hadn't left voluntarily. But even if she had left willingly with someone, she had been betrayed even more brutally than Edward.

"There was no ransom demand."

Lambert waited quietly while Edward sifted through his memories, realigning them, examining them in the light of what he had learned in the last few hours.

"Two suggestions," Edward said finally. "We need to find the former security guard at my apartment. He quit without notice and left the day before the wedding. And...maybe you'd better do this. Ask Winthrop's daughter where she got the painting."

Edward allowed his bittersweet memory only a moment's life.

"It was Jennie's wedding present to me. The last time I saw it, it was in my apartment—and so was Jennie."

Three

___

Jennie awoke while the house lay silent and still. Quietly, she made her way to the window seat and pushed open the casement window. Then, drawing her feet up onto the cushion in front of her, she rested her chin on her knees and surrendered to the gentle breeze that drifted through the window as she listened to the predawn sounds of birds searching for their breakfast.

Her world was still dark, and would be until the sun rose to lighten the dense fog of her sightlessness.

And she was alone. Still. Though surrounded by a house full of loving, caring people.

Had she always been alone?

This was the question that had filled too many of her sleepless hours in the months of her life since she had first woken up in Avalon.

She couldn't have been—not if she trusted her dreams.

But after what had happened to her, who, or what, could she trust?

The man hadn't returned by the time she had been put to bed like a child or an invalid. She didn't even know his name.

"It's better this way," Reverend Winthrop had insisted softly, patiently, and with a sadness she had not heard before in his voice. "Lucas will explain, if any explanations are necessary."

Better for whom?

Not for the first time, Jennie wondered how she looked. She knew she was shorter than most people, or at least those she had met in Avalon, whose voices all seemed to come from above her head—even Matilda's. And small. At least compared to Sheriff Lambert, who had carried her easily on more than one occasion when she was in the early stages of her recovery.

But did she look like a child? Or worse, like someone who couldn't cope with the slightest obstacle, frustration or tension?

Didn't they know? Didn't they know that her every waking hour, and too many of her sleeping ones, were filled with all of those things?

Who was the man?

Was he the tall, stern man of her dreams?

And why hadn't he returned?

"Foolish question," she whispered to the caressing breeze. He hadn't returned because Sheriff Lambert hadn't let him return—wouldn't let him until he had completely checked out the man's story and probably his life from the day he was born. The man in her dreams would not quietly tolerate that kind of inspection, that kind of doubt.

But then, the man in her dreams was just that—a figment of her imagination, created by her subconscious to ease her loneliness, to fill the awful empty hours of the night when her doubts and fears crept around her.

She heard noises through the open window, the sounds of kitchen windows on the floor below being opened and

then the robust and off-key singing of Caitlin, the Winthrops' cook and housekeeper, as she began preparations
for breakfast.

Jennie sighed and rolled her head and shoulders, hating
the tension that too often plagued her, then relinquished her
comfortable place at the window. Matilda would be coming soon to check on her, and because Jennie didn't want
the kindhearted woman to worry about how long her
charge had been awake, she eased herself back into bed and
pulled the sheet up.

Maybe today he would return, she thought as she turned
onto her side and burrowed her cheek into the softness of
the down pillows. Maybe today someone would tell her who
he was. Maybe today someone would tell her who *she* was.

Edward paced the comfortable room, impatient for dawn
to finish lighting the sky, impatient to make the telephone
calls he had promised Lambert he would wait to make.
Impatient to see Jennie again. To confront her with his accusations? To comfort her? Or just to hold the woman who
was his wife and pretend that the last six months had never
happened? To pretend that she loved him, to pretend that
he was capable of giving her the love he'd once thought she
wanted from him?

Lambert had brought him back to the outskirts of Avalon to this converted private hunting lodge last night too
late for anyone with any decent manners to go banging on
the vicar's door. The problem was, Edward wasn't feeling
particularly decent, mannerly or even civilized by that time.
What did keep him from rebelling against Lambert's edicts
was the knowledge that Jennie was probably asleep and that
she'd need all the rest and strength she could stockpile
against the time he finally told her all he knew about her
disappearance. *If* he told her the whole story.

What Edward didn't understand was why he had also
acquiesced in the matter of not contacting his office until

the next day. Postponing telling anyone until after he had
talked with Jennie, until after he'd had time to absorb at
least partially all that he had learned that day, until he'd
had time to understand at least partially all the conflicting
facts and emotions that had battered him that day, had
seemed reasonable, natural even.

But that had been while he and Lambert were seated in
front of a still-necessary fire in the huge stone fireplace
downstairs, eating the thick roast beef sandwiches the
sheriff had, with no apparent effort, convinced the innkeeper to produce long after the dining room had been
cleared. Edward had leaned back in a heavy leather chair,
poised between exhaustion and jittery nervous energy, and
accepted a welcome brandy and not so welcome advice.

He had, reluctantly, accepted the sheriff's advice,
knowing that all hell could have broken loose in his corporate offices in the twenty-four hours since he'd left San
Francisco without telling anyone where he was going.

Now, in the gray light of early morning, all that kept him
from calling Madeline was his promise to the sheriff, a
promise he was eager to be released from but that he would
honor.

At last, faint noises rose from the rooms on the ground
floor. He stopped near the window, listening, until he recognized the sounds of the lodge coming to life. At last. It
seemed hours since he had given up on sleep. He rolled his
neck and shoulders in a vain attempt to ease the tension
there, then headed for the shower in order to prepare himself for the day's events. There was no more time for delay. Jennie was waiting for him.

He stopped as he reached the bathroom door.

She was waiting for him, and she had no idea who he
was.

Once before, he'd thought that. Once before, he'd convinced himself that none of the curse of the Carlton past
could intrude on the magical time he spent with her.

Well, this time she didn't know him. Yesterday had convinced him of that much at least. But his past, with all of its suspicion and betrayal and pain, was as alive as an actual, physical person standing firmly by his side.

Laughter as soft and delicate as the melody of a distant wind chime whispered through the vicarage garden, calling to Edward and leading him deeper into the comforting, slightly shaggy maze of spring flowers and ancient trees with their tender new leaves. Leading him deeper into the maze of conflicting emotions which battered him mercilessly. Pain, anger, frustration, but most of all, weariness. Unrelenting, soul-draining weariness.

God, he was tired. Tired of being alone. Tired of always having to protect his companies, his privacy, his emotions, and even his life, from the greed that his father, and now he, seemed to attract like a powerful magnet.

For a few weeks, the woman somewhere ahead of him in the garden had made him believe in happiness and love and the goodness of others. He'd thought he wouldn't be able to survive her betrayal. And now, wounded as she was, she tempted him once again to believe, to hope that there would be someone to take away the emptiness of his life. An emptiness that before Jennie he had so completely denied, not even he had known it existed.

No!

For a moment, he thought he had moaned the word aloud, so abruptly had the denial overcome him. He stopped, slowed his breathing and listened for any outward sign that he had been heard. "No," he whispered when he at last accepted that the cry had been entirely in his mind.

But he didn't know what he was saying *no* to—the memories of his sorrow, or the memories of those first unreal weeks with Jennie.

Not again, he promised himself. He would see to her needs and he would help her recover if that was at all possible, but he wouldn't, *couldn't* open himself to the kind of pain that she had so easily, so senselessly inflicted on him. Not again.

He heard her laughter, closer now, mocking him, beckoning to him, and now it was joined by another voice, also feminine, but deeper, and, he knew, somehow, younger. The words were indistinguishable but spoken in a pleasant, bantering tone which called from Jennie another gurgle of laughter.

Edward tensed, remembering that laughter all too well. Then, forcing himself to relax, he centered his attention on the direction from which the sounds were coming and not on the bitter memories they evoked, and continued walking.

He wanted to see her once more without the presence, well-meaning or otherwise, of the vicar or the sheriff. That was why he hadn't waited for Lambert to arrive at the lodge but had requested a ride into town from the innkeeper. Requested in a calm, civil manner, but in a tone all of his employees would have recognized as a demand.

He hadn't known Jennie was in the garden. That was an unexpected bonus. When he had arrived at the vicarage, he had thought merely to take a few moments in the pleasant surroundings to collect himself and his vagrant thoughts before beginning the confrontations that were sure to mark the day.

As he walked deeper into the garden, he heard Jennie's voice join the other, and as he drew closer he began to discern words. Words, but not meaning.

"Watch out," the younger voice said breathlessly. "To the right. Higher. Quick. Up, up. Oh, drat."

"Ouch."

"Got you, did he? Darn, I'm sorry."

"Don't be," Jennie said softly. "Here, let me have him. No, no, no," she crooned. "Easy. It's time to be soft now. Easy. Easy. That's a good boy."

What the hell? Edward thought, even as he felt himself succumbing to the hypnotic temptation of Jennie's soothing voice. A lie, he reminded himself. It had all been a lie. That was all he needed to remember. And someday, some way, he would learn the reason for that lie.

He rounded a lilac bush and found her there, wearing another of those soft, flowing dresses and sitting on another stone bench. She was holding a half-grown yellow tiger-striped kitten that had stretched out in her lap and was purring loudly enough to be heard across the several feet that still separated Edward from the two women.

No, not both of them were women, he amended. The girl sitting cross-legged at Jennie's feet had several years to wait before she reached that status. All arms and long legs and huge eyes in a too-thin face, she seemed, somehow, comfortable with the spurt of growth her body had given her, comfortable with the awkward age she was passing through. Comfortable with sitting and talking and *playing* with a blind woman.

The girl saw him first and rose to her feet with awkward grace. "Jennie," she said in a hushed, protective voice. "We have company."

Jennie half rose and looked around, surely an instinctive gesture, because she looked right through him with her sightless eyes, then sighed and gave a little frown. "Who?"

"Don't know," the girl muttered. She lifted her chin and challenged him. "You'd better tell us who you are and why you're here before my dad gets here, mister."

Lambert. Edward identified who her father must be before she finished speaking. The girl's coloring was lighter and her features finer, but her mannerisms were completely and distinctly the sheriff's.

"I'm sorry I startled you—"

Jennie's frown turned into a smile of such dazzling joy it hurt him to watch. "You came back," she said breathlessly. He saw the tension drain from her as she sank back onto the bench and stroked the kitten. "I—I knew you would."

But she hadn't known. That much was as painfully clear to him as her happiness had been only moments before. And suddenly he felt this overpowering need to comfort her as she comforted the kitten. "It was late last night when we returned to Avalon—too late to disturb you."

"You went somewhere?" she asked. "You and the sheriff? Is everything all right?"

No, it wasn't, hadn't been for a long time, might never be. But that wasn't what she meant. She meant between him and the local law. "Yes," he said gently. "Everything is fine."

She extricated a hand from the cat and held it out to him. "Please," she said, her smile an invitation he had never been able to resist, "join us." She nodded toward the girl at her feet. "This is Jamie. Jamie, this is—" She stopped abruptly and looked toward him as her smile faltered. "I'm sorry. I don't know your name."

They hadn't told her. Not one thing. And in spite of the fact that she would have to know, have to confront who she was and what she had done, he couldn't tell her, either. Not now. Not without more support for her than a half-grown cat, an adolescent girl and an embittered and cynical man she had no memory of.

"I'm Edward," he said, stepping to her side and, because he couldn't help himself, taking her small hand in his.

"Edward." Her voice caressed his name as she tested the sound of it. "Edward."

Her fingers flexed in his and he felt their gentle pressure. Because he couldn't stop himself from this, either, he ran his thumb over her fingers, across the one where his rings had once dwelled, and found a ridge of tortured bone beneath delicate, pale skin.

Startled, he looked down. With a sense of relief, he found something else on which to focus, a small trail of blood oozing from a tiny wound in the fleshy pad of her thumb. "Your cat has drawn blood," he said.

"Let me see," Jamie said.

The girl pushed her way between them and grabbed Jennie's hand. "Oh, darn," she said. "I'm sorry. Heathcliff's had his shots so that—"

"It's all right," Jennie told her.

"But—"

"It's all right, Jamie," she repeated again. "He was just playing."

"Something to clean it with would be in order," Edward told the girl.

"And I'm supposed to believe it's all right to leave you alone with her?"

"Yes," Jennie insisted softly. "It is. And no, I don't need any first aid."

Jamie studied him with Lambert's wary, suspicious eyes. And then, because Edward couldn't stop this, either, another, darker thought intruded. *Meggie*. Was this how his sister would have been at Jamie's age? Tall, yes. That had always been a given. But would she have been poised and comfortable with herself beneath the mantle of security Jamie wore so casually? Or would she have been awkward and at war with a body growing too fast for her heart and mind to keep pace with?

This was something else that Jennie had done to him. She had drawn him out of the shell he had so painstakingly erected and laid open wounds he had thought long healed.

Forcing himself away from those thoughts, he smiled at the girl. "You might as well tell Reverend Winthrop I'm here, even though I'm pretty sure the innkeeper has already called your father and told him that he brought me into town."

Jamie grinned at him. "It's a small town. It's either great or a really big pain depending on your attitude and what you want to keep secret."

"Antiseptic," he reminded her.

"Yeah, sure." She grinned again. "Just as soon as you promise me you're not an ax murderer or an escapee from a mental institution."

"Jamie!" Jennie drew in a shocked breath.

"I promise," he told her.

Again she studied him. "He's gorgeous," she said before turning and starting along the brick path that led to the vicarage. Now it was Edward's turn to draw in a breath. "Maybe you'd better keep him," she called over her shoulder as she broke into a run.

Jennie sighed and shrugged, as if in apology. "She's— exuberant," she said, patting the seat beside her. "Please. Please sit down. I'm getting a catch in my neck from looking up at you."

He shot her a quick glance before he realized she had tilted her head to one side, much as she had always done to look up at him, but had cocked her head so that the shell of her ear, not her eyes, turned toward him. Listening. Yes. Listening, not watching.

"You are very tall, aren't you?" she asked.

"Yes." Hesitant, he dropped onto the bench beside her. He didn't want this, he told himself, didn't want the closeness, didn't want even the appearance of intimacy, of sharing. *Didn't he?* Wasn't wanting all those things what had brought him almost to the point of not being able to go on?

"You're up very early," he said, to make noise, to fill the void so that other words, words he knew he shouldn't say, wouldn't fill it instead.

"Am I?" Jennie lifted one small shoulder in a delicate shrug. "It seems as though the sun has been up for hours."

"You can tell?"

"Yes." She raised her face toward the dappled sunlight. "Daylight is warmer. Morning has an expectancy to it, different sounds, even a different smell. And it's not as dark."

Her smile faltered. "I hate the dark."

She looked down at the cat and began stroking his yellow fur. "You're not going to tell me anything, are you?"

What must it be like to live in a world of darkness, not knowing who you were or where you'd been, not remembering a talent that had given meaning to your life, knowing that the only persons you could depend upon were truly strangers? Edward couldn't imagine. Nor, looking at this fragile woman, did he want to.

"Perhaps we had better go back to the house," he said.

She sighed and stood. "If you'll carry Heathcliff," she said, "I can place my hand on your arm for guidance. He's Jamie's," she continued when Edward hesitated. "We left his carrier at the house, and he can't be left here to get lost."

The cat seemed to glare at him as Edward reached for him, apparently not at all happy at being transferred from Jennie's arms to those of a strange man. Edward wasn't particularly happy about the thought of cat hair on his dark slacks, but he reached over and scratched a spot just below the cat's chin. Heathcliff bared two sharp teeth in what appeared to be a grin, and Edward lifted him from Jennie's arms.

"Thank you," she said, slipping her hand into the crook of his elbow. "I don't need much help, just a little guidance." She chuckled ruefully. "And maybe a warning or two if you see a tree root."

She was trying so hard to be valiant that for a moment she had him convinced that he hadn't seen disappointment in her eyes when he'd silently refused her request for information, that he hadn't seen the frustration in her eyes when she admitted to needing help. He shifted Heathcliff to his shoulder and released him just long enough to clasp his hand briefly over Jennie's.

She smiled up at him. "Reverend Winthrop has been talking about getting me a dog," she said. "One to help me get around with some sense of independence. Did I have a dog when—when you knew me?"

Did she have a dog? Visions of Jennie darted through his memory: Jennie, running along the beach, barefoot with her gorgeous hair flying behind her. Jennie dancing with absolute abandon at a street festival in the campy neighborhood she called home. Jennie, paint-spattered and exultant, standing before dozens of misty, otherworldly canvases that she had created and putting the finishing touch to the one she would give him.

The one that now hung in the vicar's parlor.

"No," he said. "No dog."

She absorbed that for a moment. "It's just as well I don't have one," she said finally, lightly. "I'd probably spoil it rotten, ruin all its training and wind up being pulled all over the garden.

"Was I—was I always blind?"

"Jennie—"

"I'm sorry. I know." Her voice caught, and when she continued she seemed more subdued than at any time since he'd met her. "I know you don't want to answer questions. But I have so many of them. I think I must not have been blind always," she told him. "Because in my mind, I see things. People. Plants. Animals. Landscapes. I couldn't do that if I'd never seen them, could I? Or maybe what I think I'm seeing is only my—my impression of how they should look, not like they really look at all—"

Edward stopped and turned to face her, blocking her path. With the damned cat clawing its way up his shoulder, there was no way he could do what he sensed he should do: take Jennie in his arms and comfort her, tell her that everything would be all right, tell her what she wanted to know.

"No," he said. "When I first met you, you were sighted."

"Then, how—"

With his one free hand, he traced the delicate line of her jaw. "And that's why I didn't want to start answering questions. Because you do have so many. And I don't have answers for them all."

"But—"

"No," he said softly, wrapping his own pain in protective layers and pushing it aside so that, for now, he could try to deal with Jennie's. "Not until you have Reverend Winthrop with you. And maybe that woman who was with you yesterday, the grandmotherly—"

"Matilda."

"Yes. Her."

Matilda wasn't present; Jennie banished her from the parlor with loving kindness, then stood at the mantel beneath the painting she couldn't see. She listened quietly to the abbreviated story Edward chose to tell her then faced him, the sheriff and vicar with quiet dignity.

"I'm your wife," she repeated. "I disappeared on our wedding day. I apparently have—had—some professional status. I've been here for six months and no one—*no one*—has been looking for me?"

"Miss Jennie," Lambert said in his soft drawl. "Mr. Carlton had no reason to look for you in New Mexico."

Edward shot him a glance, which Lambert met, daring him to contradict him.

"I see," Jennie said.

But she didn't understand, Edward knew, any more than he understood why he had stopped himself from telling her about the note she had left him, about the missing bonds and about her emptied studio.

"Excuse me." Jennie looked around the room as though she could see each person, each item of furniture, and was looking for a safe place. "I—" Her voice caught, her chin lifted in a defiant gesture that was so—so *Jennie* that Edward wanted to wrap her in his arms and be that safe place for her. What kept him from crossing the room to her was knowing that once she remembered her past, she would realize that she didn't want him, for any reason.

"I have to go to my room now," she said. "I have to think about this."

"Miss Jennie, you ought to be with people who—"

"No, Sheriff Lambert. Please don't tell me what I ought to do. Reverend Winthrop, would you show me to my room?"

Sheriff Lambert. Reverend Winthrop. Those were the persons she turned to. Not him. But hadn't Edward expected that? He watched silently as the vicar lifted Jennie's hand to his arm and guided her from the room.

Lambert turned to him. "You didn't tell her."

Edward shook his head. Even he didn't understand why he hadn't. "What good would it have done?"

"What will you do now?"

"Call my office, see what disasters have occurred since I dropped out of sight, start the process of moving some of my key people here."

"You could just go home."

"And leave her? Now? After opening her up to all sorts of questions? I don't think so, Sheriff."

"Wasn't that what you had originally planned to do before you ever came to Avalon—see her again, then leave?"

Damn him for being so perceptive. Edward walked to the mantel and looked at the painting of the *Lady B.* "Plans change," he said softly, thinking of other plans, of other times. "Plans change."

Four

"Where are you, Edward? My God, we've been frantic since we traced your plane to the El Paso airport and found you'd just dropped off the face of the earth."

Frantic, perhaps. But Madeline's words were more a chastisement for leaving his staff without their leader than an outpouring of worry over him. In the ten years she'd been with him, he'd never doubted her loyalty to him personally, but he knew her greater loyalty lay with the company. Which was precisely what made her such a good administrative assistant.

Edward leaned back against the headboard of his bed in the lodge and for the first time considered why he'd always thought that quality such an asset. "I've found Jennie."

Edward's softly spoken words stopped her torrent. He'd occasionally wondered what it would take to flap the unflappable Madeline. Now as he listened to the silence, he knew.

"It's true, then. What...what does she have to say for herself?" Madeline asked.

"Nothing. She remembers nothing about why she left or how she got here."

More silence. The highly sensitive telephone picked up the sounds of Madeline's breathing and nothing else—none of the sounds of a busy workday that should have intruded even in her private office.

"How—how convenient for her," she said. "I'll contact Fallon immediately. I'm sure he will be happy to know where to serve her with your divorce papers. And I'm sure he would tell you to have as little contact with her as possible. When can we expect your return? There are several matters pending—"

"Madeline."

She stopped in midsentence and waited.

To give Madeline credit, she had never intruded on his private life, except where Jennie was concerned. And only after Jennie left had she done much more than insist he be sure of what he was doing, that he be sure of Jennie's motives. Fallon, his attorney, had been much more suspicious of the young artist, her motives and her avowed love for the keeper of the Carlton millions. It was Fallon who had insisted upon and prepared the prenuptial agreement Jennie had signed. But since the day Jennie disappeared, Madeline had dragged out all the suspicions she apparently had been keeping to herself and had urged him regularly to take all legal steps necessary to protect himself from any claims Jennie might make on him in the future.

Well, she had claims, whether or not Madeline or Fallon, or even Edward liked it.

"No divorce," he said. "And I'm not coming back. At least not right away."

"*No divorce?* Edward. After all she's put you through? And what do you mean, you're not returning? Do you know what that can do to our schedules?"

Schedules be damned, he thought. But he kept all emotion from his voice. "Jennie needs me here."

"Jennie needs you? *Jennie* needs you?" Madeline's voice raised with a lack of control he had never heard in it, before lowering again to the calm—well, maybe not quite calm—tone he associated with her.

"You owe her nothing after what she's done to you," Madeline insisted. "Now you're going to stick around some little backwater in—where? Where exactly did she light, Edward? And how do you expect to run Carlton Enterprises from wherever it is while you baby-sit someone so—so—"

"With the help of my staff," he said curtly. Enough was enough. Even though she had often seemed invaluable, it was time to remind her just who did run Carlton Enterprises.

"I'm in Avalon, New Mexico. Have someone pick up the plane in El Paso. I'll want Tim out here as quickly as possible to set up a field office, while you decide which files to bring and which to delegate. I'll want you here with me, Madeline, in no more than a week. In the meantime, express me a fax machine and a laptop and anything that can't wait for my attention."

"You're jeopardizing everything, Edward. And for what? For a woman who has proven how unreliable she is?"

"For my wife, Madeline."

"Your *wife?*" she repeated incredulously. "How can you say that? How can you think you owe her any loyalty? Obviously, she didn't mean the vows she made."

"Maybe not," he admitted, "but when I made those same vows, I did mean them. And until Jennie is in a position to explain or defend, or even to admit, what happened, I intend to keep them."

* * *

Edward found her in the garden. Alone. But this time he saw no smile, no animation in her gamine features. He heard no laughter.

She sat on the same bench where he had found her the first day, and for the first time since he had met her months before, she seemed drawn into herself. Guarded. Protective. And so very much alone.

Who was he, Jennie? Edward questioned silently. *Who did you leave with? Who did you love more than me? Trust more than me? And who betrayed that trust?*

And why do I still care?

Because he did. In spite of the pain of her betrayal. In spite of the hell of the past six months. Watching her silently as she sat on the garden bench, he could almost imagine that the world had never intruded on the interlude he had shared with a laughing, loving sprite.

This morning, the scents and soft noises of the garden, the warmth of the sun on her face, brought Jennie no joy. She'd told herself over and over during the past months that somewhere there was someone who loved her, someone who was searching for her, someone who would find her. And on the day that happened, even though she had never voiced the hope, she would remember the past, remember the love.

She didn't.

And perhaps it was just as well. Edward—*her husband*—hadn't been searching for her. Wouldn't be here now if not for Reverend Winthrop's loving interference. Why not? Why on earth would a man not search for his new bride? Especially someone like Edward Carlton?

Granted, she had only spent a few minutes with him, but in those minutes he had seemed—had seemed—what? Stalwart. An old-fashioned word but one which seemed to fit the man who had refused to talk with her until she had others around her to give her support should she need it. Stalwart and true.

So why wouldn't he have looked for her? Unless—unless *she* had done something.

Jennie gripped the edge of the bench, suddenly chilled in spite of the warmth of the sunlight on her face. She didn't think she would ever have intentionally hurt someone, especially someone she had promised to love and to cherish. But if not that, what?

And how, oh, God, how had she gotten from being an artist who was building a reputation for subtle and sensitive work to someone who saw color and form only in her dreams? From a wedding in San Francisco to a mountain in New Mexico?

She sensed a presence nearby and for a moment the fear and uncertainty of her last question twisted inside her. Until she remembered she was in the vicar's walled garden, safe from intrusion. Until she noticed the faint yet enticing aromas of soap, shampoo and man that she had been so aware of yesterday. Until she identified her visitor.

"Edward," she said calmly, hoping she betrayed none of her fears.

"Yes."

She heard his footsteps on the brick walk as he drew closer. She scooted to one side to make room for him on the bench and gestured for him to join her.

"Are you sure?"

She heard hesitation in his voice, an uncertainty of his welcome, and tried, tried so hard, to find a smile for him.

"Please," she said.

He sat stiffly beside her on the bench, and she felt his reluctance, or maybe even his inability, to relax in her presence and knew that her last assumptions about herself had been closer to truth than she ever would have wanted.

"Edward?" she asked softly, because she knew now she must ask. "You didn't try to find me, did you?"

He drew himself even more upright and sat silently beside her for much too long. "No," he said finally, not even attempting to deny that he hadn't.

"Why?" she asked, trying not to let this betrayal hurt so much, trying not to let her tears force themselves free. And then, knowing that she had to ask this, too, had to know, she made herself speak softly and calmly. "What—what did I do to you?"

His tension thrummed between them, palpable and real. Tension and frustration. Anger and betrayal. Pain and a frightening, controlled calm.

"You left me," he told her.

Never would she have suspected that answer. Never could she believe it. Not her. Not the Jennie she had known for six months. One didn't make lifetime promises lightly. And having made them, one didn't break them.

"Why?"

She felt the soft stir of air as he lifted his hand, as he held it close to her cheek but didn't touch her, as he lowered it to the bench. "Ah, Jennie," he said softly, letting his pain seep through, "if we had the answer to that question, we'd have more answers than either one of us could deal with right now."

He was coming. Two days had passed since Edward had left her sitting in the garden. Two days for Jennie to wonder at the pain in his voice when he told her she'd left him. Two days for her to wonder how she could have done such a thing. To wonder how he could bear to look at her if she had.

Now Dr. Freede had told her, and, against her wishes, had told him, that spending time together might—might be the catalyst that could help her remember how she had come to Avalon. And Sheriff Lambert, her friend, the traitor, the dear, had insisted that Edward do more than watch over her from the safe distance of the Avalon Lodge.

Too restless to wait quietly in her room for his arrival, Jennie started downstairs, only to be halted by the sounds of heavy footsteps in the foyer and the opening of the front door.

"Carlton."

It was Sheriff Lambert's voice, but in a tone he had never used with her. Startled, but even more curious, she paused on the landing.

"Lambert."

Edward's voice was every bit as stiff and strained as the sheriff's.

Aware that all they had to do was look up to see her paused there, but unwilling to leave and not hear the outcome of this strange confrontation, Jennie gathered the yards of the flowing fabric of her skirt and settled down on the top stair, her head cocked slightly to eavesdrop unabashedly.

She heard the second set of footsteps enter the foyer.

"You've moved your office?" Edward's voice carried subtle sarcasm but also a deeper, proprietary tone out of keeping with the vicar's pleasant home.

"Just doing my job." Lucas Lambert's gravelly southern drawl had an edge to it Jennie had never heard before. She wrapped an arm around one of the banister rails and rested her cheek against the cool, polished wood.

"Which is?"

"Seeing that Jennie doesn't get hurt any more than she already has been."

The front door shut with a thud that spoke of a barely controlled slam. "And you still think that I would hurt her?"

"There are different kinds of pain, Carlton. No. I don't think you had anything to do with her physical injuries. I've told you that. But I do think you have the power to hurt her greatly."

"So I should just leave her to your tender mercies? No, Lambert. You're forgetting—Jennie is my wife."

"No. You're the one who forgot that, who forgot where his loyalties lay, who accepted at face value something so utterly preposterous that I had to ask myself why—why any so-called intelligent man, and you are purported to be extremely capable, would allow himself to believe what is so patently untrue. So I dug a little deeper into your background."

"My background is none of your business."

"And besides, it's ancient history, right?" The sheriff sighed. "Mr. Carlton, I don't want to open old wounds. I know they must still be painful no matter how old they are. But you have to know that this kind of horror can be repeated, that there is no limit of one to a customer with terrorism—"

"Enough!" Edward said with chilling calm, stopping the sheriff's softly spoken words and leaving Jennie leaning against the banister, listening—listening with all her heart to learn what had once hurt the man who said he was her husband. "Enough. What happened twenty-five years ago can have no bearing on what's happening now. And I repeat, it's none of your business."

Surely that tone would have stopped most people—Jennie knew that its brittle chill would have stopped her, but apparently it didn't frighten Lucas Lambert.

"Wrong," he said. "What happens to Avalon and the people in it, including your wife, *is* my business."

"Then instead of concerning yourself with my past, you should get busy and find out who pushed her off that mountain."

Pushed her off the mountain?

Jennie's hand clenched on the banister rail as a startled gasp escaped from her. Pushed her? She'd fallen, hadn't she? Wasn't that what she'd been told? Or had she been told anything? Had she just assumed she fell? Then why, now, did Edward's words seem so true? Why, now, did she feel so threatened?

"Miss Jennie—"

"My God. Haven't you told her—"

She heard their words through the waves of unwelcome and unexpected terror that crowded against her in the dark, through the words that sprang unwanted from the darkness of her memory.

No! You can't do this. You'll never get away with it.

Shut up, bitch. You have to die. You know too much.

Know what? She knew nothing. *Nothing!*

"Jennie?"

She was on her feet. How had she managed that? She felt herself swaying. Felt the thickness of fear in her throat. Felt the futility of running, but knew she had to... had to—

"Jennie."

He caught her. Edward caught her as she fell, and lifted her in his arms. Safe. She hated the pitiful little whimper that broke from her; she hated the weakness that threatened to overwhelm her. And she knew—knew as she let herself drift toward the welcoming darkness—that she had nothing to fear as long as he held her.

Safe. Oh, yes. At last she was safe.

Her room was a bower of pastel and watercolor prints, a perfect setting for the delicate vision Jennie presented. Edward carried her to a chintz-covered chaise longue and hesitated there. He didn't want to hold her any longer than necessary—holding her, remembering, was too painful—but perversely, he couldn't bear to move her head from his shoulder, to release his arms from around her and lay her down on the chaise. Too long. It had been too long since he had held her.

"Here," Lambert said, reaching to take Jennie from him.

The hell he would. Edward glared at the sheriff. "Get a doctor."

Lambert gave him a hard, steady stare, nodded once and strode from the room. Edward glanced down at the pale chaise before bending to place Jennie on it. What was he doing here? What was she doing here in this stage set for a fragile, broken flower? The Jennie he knew would have surrounded herself with color—reds and purples, bright blues, vibrant oranges.

The Jennie he knew . . .

But he didn't know her, did he? And he didn't want to, did he? Not after what she had done.

But his hand lingered on her cheek as he knelt beside her, even as he heard footsteps entering the room.

Her eyelids fluttered once. "Renn?" she whispered.

Renn. The name only she had ever called him. The name she had given him in teasing and, he'd thought, love. Renn. A name from a past that was all illusion. He felt his heart clench at the painful memories, even as his fingers gentled on her cheek. "I'm here, Jennie. I'm here."

Her hand came up to clasp his, her breathing deepened and she smiled as she slid deeper into whatever darkness claimed her. Edward became aware of other people in the room and looked up to find Lambert and Matilda Higgins standing beside him. The woman wore a strange, yet satisfied, expression.

"That's the name," she said softly. "I knew I hadn't misheard."

"Renberg, of course," Lambert said.

"What name?" Edward asked softly but with the authority of command.

Lambert smiled grimly. "The name she called out when she first regained consciousness. Her first word, apparently her first thought was for you. Tell me, Carlton, does that sound like a woman who has run away from someone she meant only to use?"

Edward felt himself blanching. No. No, it didn't. But if she hadn't left him, then what had happened? And why? There had been no ransom note—God knew, he had faced too many hours in the past waiting for one of those—no messages at all, other than those he had believed to be from her, no indication that anything was other than it appeared.

Jennie. He faced the image of Jennie, alone and injured, calling out for him while he accepted the delivery of her mangled rings, stripped of their stones, while he girded his defenses by reading and rereading the note she had left him. He felt those defenses crumbling around him now. Lies? Had it all been lies?

By whom?

And why?

And oh, God, if they were lies, could she ever forgive him for believing them? Could he ever forgive himself?

Jennie struggled up through the darkness, fighting the stabbing pain in her head and the by-now-familiar disorientation of time and place. She heard the soft sounds of steady breathing from nearby and tensed, then forced herself to relax so she could identify the source. Not a stranger. And not Matilda. For now she knew where she was, and who should be with her. She recognized the subtle woodland scent of after-shave mingled with the luxurious brand of soap offered by the Avalon Lodge.

Edward.

Sleeping?

Had it been that long then, since—since what? What had brought on this latest attack?

Quietly she raised herself to one elbow, feeling the soft slide of the light woven coverlet as it slipped around her, and reached for the small table beside the chaise. Matilda would have left something there for the headache; she always did.

Abruptly, Edward's breathing changed. She heard the sounds of him moving in the chair and then felt his hand on hers as she reached for the capsules and water.

Now Jennie tensed beneath his touch. Familiar and yet not familiar. Welcome and yet alien. Gentle in spite of the strength she sensed in his large hand. Inspiring memories, or perhaps only imaginings, not of happenings but of sensations.

While she tried to sort though those sensations, he turned her hand in his and placed two capsules in it, then closed her fingers over the medication. She sighed, swallowed the pills with water from the glass he handed her, then sank back against the lace-trimmed pillows.

"Does this happen often?" he asked.

Fainting? No. Panic? No. Flashes of memory too painful to be borne—because now she remembered the secret Edward's angry words to Sheriff Lambert had revealed and the answering flicker of memory they caused? No.

"The headaches?" she said quietly, trying not to wince as her words reverberated through her head. "Yes."

She closed her eyes and felt blessed relief as he draped a damp cloth across her forehead. She smiled her thanks but didn't attempt to speak again. Apparently sensing her discomfort, neither did he, until several minutes had passed and she sighed as her tension and pain finally eased.

"Better?" he asked.

"Yes."

"But not gone?"

She shook her head, defying the small bursts of pressure and pain. "They linger, sometimes for hours."

"Then I'll leave you to rest."

"No, please." She put her hand out and miraculously found his. "I—I don't want to be alone."

She heard disbelief in his voice. "Jennie, you're not alone. You have a whole town at your command."

She fought her disappointment and tried to make him understand. "Yes, but they're not—they're not really mine, you know..."

Too late she remembered their last conversation. Too late she remembered that *she* had left him alone, and not just for an afternoon. Too late she remembered that he wasn't hers, either—if he ever truly had been. She released her grip on him but was unable to drop her hand from his. "I'm sorry. I have no right—"

"Don't you?" Now his hand tightened on hers. "I wonder..."

Something—but what?—had happened since last they talked. Something to change his utter conviction that she had abandoned him. She heard this much in his voice but no hint of an explanation. And he offered none.

"Rest now, Jennie," he said softly. "I'll be here for you. At least for a while."

But at what cost to yourself? she wondered as she sank back into the pillows, her hand still clasped in his, because she heard the strain in his voice.

Jennie still slept when Mrs. Higgins brought Edward a tight, terse message that his people had begun arriving at the airport.

"Go on, now, and get them started on whatever they need to be doing," she told him. "I'll stay with Jennie."

"I said I'd be here for her," he said, telling himself that his promise was the only reason he didn't want to leave Jennie defenseless in sleep.

Mrs. Higgins's worn expression softened. She smiled fondly, but not at him, he realized, even as she shook her head, and he wondered what had brought about this change in her. Though never overly friendly toward him, she had been open if not accepting. Now that openness was hidden behind a stiff formality out of keeping with her pleasant, grandmotherly appearance. "She'll understand. Jennie always understands."

Yes. She did. Jennie's capacity for understanding and accepting his needs and the needs of others was one of the first things he had noticed about her. After he had recovered from the blow her delicate beauty and unaffected sensuality had dealt him. After he had been able to think about anything other than how much he wanted to drag this woman off to his cave and never let her out of his sight again. After he had begun to hope that she might return the love he was finally beginning to learn how to give.

"Mr. Carlton?"

Edward brought his attention back to the present and stretched up out of the chair.

"Mr. Carlton. I'll take good care of her. I promise."

"I know you will, Mrs. Higgins," he said. "Just as I know that you have in the past."

Mrs. Higgins gave a soft, short sigh, but her look told him she had thawed toward him, at least slightly.

"Is there something wrong, Mrs. Higgins? Something I ought to know about?"

She hesitated, but after a moment she smiled ruefully at him. "No," she said. "Nothing for you to be concerned about. Now, you'd best hurry. That Miss Harrison sounded awfully impatient."

Madeline? Madeline was here already? For someone who hadn't wanted to come, she had certainly managed to get everything in order in record time. Edward caught his thoughts. Wasn't that exactly what he paid her to do?

And if he expected to be able to continue paying her and the rest of his staff, he had better begin paying attention to his business.

Unable to stop himself, though, before he left Jennie alone, he leaned over her. God help him, he thought, because he couldn't help himself. Not where Jennie was concerned. Not now. Maybe not ever. And then, because he couldn't stop himself, once again he touched his fingers to Jennie's softly parted lips. *I'll be back,* he told her silently, even as he wondered whether his words were promise or threat.

Five

Avalon's airport lay nestled on a plateau just below the town, an Art Deco punctuation to the nineteenth-century village. Lambert had shown him the drive to the airport that first afternoon, but Edward had had no time to admire the trendy modernity of the buildings then, nor did he now.

He parked in front of the large black marble-and-tile facade and entered the building through etched glass and brass doors, pushing away the thought that the people of Avalon hadn't spared cost when it came to building their town.

Madeline stood near the single, black marble counter in earnest conversation with the uniformed man behind the desk. Beside her sat one wheeled carrier containing two locked portable file boxes and a black soft-sided case for a portable computer. She turned at the sound of his footsteps.

"I'm sorry to bother you, Mr. Carlton, but thank you for coming so promptly," she said, smiling. "This lovely facility had only one car available, but Mr. Albright here has promised to have more available by tomorrow. I sent Tim and the others on because I knew you'd want them to get started while we go over some of the projects we're currently working on."

Edward glanced at the man behind the counter to see that he wore the look of someone mildly stunned, a frequent enough reaction to Madeline Harrison's beauty. Though only distantly related through a second cousin, Madeline had inherited the Carlton height and dark hair and eyes, but with a finer bone structure and fair, almost translucent skin. She didn't use her beauty to get what she wanted, exactly; it was just there, as it had been since he first met her when she was a child. As was her keen intellect and a will, though usually kept hidden, that he knew to be almost as strong as his own.

Albright hadn't had a chance. If he'd had to walk to the nearest town to get her a car, he probably would have.

"Thank you," Edward said to the man. He glanced back at Madeline. "Are you ready?"

She laughed softly and nodded toward the wheeled carrier. Silently and efficiently, a porter appeared, taking control of the carrier and following at a discreet distance.

"Mr. Albright was telling me some of the history of Avalon," she said as they waited for the porter to load the files in the rear of Edward's rented Jeep. "Did you know it was founded by a group of Englishmen who came over in the last century and decided that as second sons they had more of a future here?"

Edward nodded distractedly, found a tip for the porter and opened the car door for Madeline. When he joined her in the interior of the vehicle, she was still wearing her smile, but it faded when they drove through the gate.

"My God, Edward, what is this place?" she asked. "I feel as though I'm in some sort of time warp. The entire time I was waiting for you, I had the strangest impression I was on a set for a PBS "Mystery" episode and that any moment Diana Rigg would walk out from behind one of those Art Deco facades to explain the plot."

Edward laughed easily. How nice it was to be on familiar footing once again, with someone he understood and who understood him. "Wait until you see the rest of it," he told her.

The road wound around a final curve and began its ascent to the town.

"Good Lord," Madeline said on an indrawn breath. "Those second sons didn't just not go back to merry old England, they brought it over here."

He chuckled. "Now," he said, "while we're alone, as you so obviously planned, tell me why you're here days earlier than I expected you, and why you couldn't ride to the lodge with the rest of the crew but had to set aside this private time."

He waited in silence for several seconds. Finally, he glanced her way to see her folding her hands in her lap and straightening in the seat.

"I was worried about you."

Her response was about what he had expected, but that didn't make it any more welcome. "I'm a big boy, Madeline," he told her, a variation of words he had said to her many times. "I have been for years. I can take care of myself."

"Can you?" she asked. "I'm not sure. At least not where Jennie is concerned. She can hurt you. She *has* hurt you. I don't want that to happen again."

"Jennie won't hurt me."

"Won't she? Her entire history is filled with people she's hurt. Did you know she was adopted? And that days before the adoption was to be completed, she was taken back to the agency? Did you know that she almost ruined the career of a professor at the college she attended? Or that she's moved three times in the five years since she graduated? Why would she do that, Edward, unless she was leaving someone else she'd used?''

''You had her investigated? When?''

Madeline sighed. ''I knew you'd react this way. All righteous and indignant.''

''When, Madeline?''

''Before you married her. I hoped I'd be able to talk you out of it, but you were so determined—''

''And you never showed me the report?''

''What good would it have done then?''

''And later?''

She reached as though to touch his arm, but dropped her hand. ''Later it didn't seem necessary. You were going through enough hell without my raking up her past for you.''

He nodded his head toward the boxes in the back. ''I suppose the report is in one of those files.''

''No.''

He heard the slight hesitation in her voice.

''Why not?''

''I meant to bring it,'' she told him. ''If anything will bring you to your senses, that might, but when I opened the folder where I'd filed it, I found—I found nothing. Absolutely nothing.''

He could have asked if she'd misfiled it, or he could have asked if someone in the office had accidentally misplaced it, but he didn't. He knew Madeline too well to doubt she'd been anything other than careful with an item so potentially damaging.

''Who did the work?'' he asked.

''Slater.''

Edward nodded. Slater was good. Very good. ''And how long has the report been missing?''

"I don't know. I haven't looked at it since—since the night before your wedding."

He nodded. "You didn't tell security?"

"No. I wanted to talk with you first."

They'd reached the lodge. Edward braked to a stop in front of the double oak doors and sat silently for a moment, attempting to fit this latest piece into a puzzle that still made no sense.

"And now you have talked to me," he said when he saw the innkeeper open one of the doors and start toward them. He opened his own door, stepped out and waited while Madeline oversaw the unloading of the files.

"Call Slater," he told her as she turned to enter the inn. "Tell him to fax me— No," he said as he walked to the driver's side door and opened it. "Tell him to courier me a copy of the report, to my attention only."

"But our conference," Madeline said as she realized he was leaving.

"Later, Madeline. Make that one call, then you can rest, explore the town, or organize your work. I'll be back later."

"Edward—"

"Later," he said, this time in a tone she knew not to question.

Later, he thought as he drove away from the lodge. Later. After—after what?

After he saw Jennie again. He had the answer to his question the moment he found himself on the street that ran in front of the vicarage.

After he assured himself she was all right.

After he tried once again to see any trace of the woman Madeline had described, of the woman who could have left him the way she had, in Jennie's fragile beauty. Honest and loving, the vicar had called her. Open and innocent. Was she? *God, if you're really there,* he thought, praying for the first time in more years than he ever wanted to remember, *tell me. Is she?*

A battered black Rolls Royce pulled away from the curb in front of the vicar's home just as Edward reached it. He almost smiled at another example of the town's casual acceptance of things someone outside this village would quite possibly revere until he noticed the doctor's insignia on the rear tag.

Reverend Winthrop met him at the door. "She's all right, Mr. Carlton," he said without waiting for Edward to ask. "Mrs. Higgins became a little concerned, that's all. But Dr. Freede assured all of us that there are no new complications. But why don't you go on up and assure yourself?"

Jennie had moved from the chaise longue to the wide, cushioned window seat. She sat with her cheek resting against the facing of the open window, her delicate features tense with some dark emotion, as a light breeze teased her short curls.

Edward paused in the doorway, but some sound he made must have alerted her to his presence. She turned toward him, and a questioning smile instantly erased all trace of what had been troubling her. "Mrs. Higgins?" she asked. "Matilda?"

"No," he told her.

Her smile faded. She sighed deeply, leaned her head back against the window facing and closed her eyes, letting him glimpse again the emotion that troubled her. "I suppose they sent for you, too," she said softly. "I'm sorry. I really am all right."

"Are you?" Not waiting for her to invite him into the room, because it was quite possible she wasn't going to, Edward walked to her side. "You weren't all right when I left."

She lifted her chin in a gesture so familiar to him, the months of separation melted away. "Nevertheless," she said, "they shouldn't have bothered you. And they shouldn't have bothered Dr. Freede."

"No one bothered me, Jennie," he told her. "I came back because I wanted to. No," he said, needing to be as honest with her as he wanted to believe she was with him. "I came back because I had to. Now, tell me why Mrs. Higgins sent for the doctor."

Jennie's mouth twisted in a rueful smile. "She thought I might be remembering."

Edward held himself still. Dr. Freede had told him her memory could return spontaneously, without warning. Or never. "Were you?"

She shook her head and once again leaned back against the window. "A few words that could be memory or imagination. An emotion. Nothing more."

"Are you sure?"

She turned her beautiful dark eyes toward him—eyes that seemed to look through him to his soul but which saw nothing but shadow. "Edward, how do I look?"

"You must know you're a beautiful woman."

She shook her head in a quick negative gesture. "Thank you, I think. But that's not what I meant. Do I look— competent?"

"I don't understand."

"Do I look as though I'm not capable of knowing when I do or don't feel well, when I'm hungry, when I want to rest or be alone, and when I need to be around other people—"

"Jennie..."

"Marianna Richards is the lovely woman who picks out my clothes for me, because obviously I can't do that. She comes by every morning to make sure that I'm dressed correctly—she doesn't say that's why she comes, but it is. She'd put makeup on me if I'd let her. Matilda—Mrs. Higgins—has her own home, but she has been with me every day, all day, until I go to bed at night, since I first woke up in the hospital.

"Mrs. Winthrop and Caitlin are forever bringing me herb teas and little treats to tempt me to eat, and if I let them know I'm the slightest bit sad, they tell Reverend Winthrop. I know they do, because it's only minutes before he's with me, sharing one of his wonderful insights. I don't know how to live with that kind of unselfishness. It's overwhelming, and it's—it's—"

"They love you, Jennie. This entire town loves you."

"Do they?" She bit her lower lip and rocked forward slightly, then back. "Or do they love what they've made of me? Would they love me if they knew the real me, Edward?" Her voice broke. "Would anyone?"

Yes! he wanted to tell her. Anyone. Everyone. He would. *If she were—*

She sighed. "Your silence is my answer, then, isn't it? Was I so awful? You loved me—or did you? No one looked for me. No one came."

"I came, Jennie."

"Yes," she said, once again biting her lower lip. "You came. But why?"

Why indeed? He'd thought he knew his reasons, but that was before he'd seen her again. Why? There was only one answer, and that was one he'd given earlier in response to another question. "I came because I had to."

She smiled at him then, a sad little smile that tore at his heart. "Take me away from here," she said softly.

He wanted to. God, how he wanted to. He wanted her alone with him, with no barriers and no secrets between them. He wanted to go back to the weeks of their courtship when she had coaxed and bullied and coerced him into laughing, when the innocence he had seen in her had seduced him into giving away his heart. He wanted to go back to the day of their wedding when he had accepted the gift of her innocent, untutored body. But more than any of those things, now he wanted the truth, and the truth could not be learned by running away from it.

He shook his head before he remembered she couldn't see the gesture. "I've promised the sheriff I won't do that. At least not until he and I both have some answers about how you came to be here."

Her eyes widened, and she swallowed once, a reflexive gesture that drew his eyes to her slender throat. "I—I didn't mean away from Avalon," she said softly. "At least I don't think I did. I meant—I thought I meant—away from this house, out into the sunshine, just for a while."

With no protest, except an admonition from Mrs. Winthrop for them to wait while she fetched Jennie a sweater, they left the house. Edward lifted Jennie's hand to his arm, and she smiled at him, as though welcoming his guidance. Did she have any idea how much it cost him to feel her touch on his arm, to remember other times, other touches, and yet give her no more than the slight guidance she claimed to need?

What would he do if he gave in to the emotions that battered him when her fingers rested gently on his arm? Take her into his arms and frighten her with the passion she had always aroused in him simply by being Jennie? Hold her safe from the world? Or shake her with a violence that frightened even him until she told him the truth about what really happened the day she left?

On the brick path that led to the garden, she stopped and lifted her face to the sun, to the warmth and the light, then turned to him.

"Could we really play hooky?" she asked.

Edward hesitated, not knowing if what she wanted to do would cause Lambert in both his roles, sheriff and guardian, to swoop down upon them. He'd face Lambert the sheriff without a qualm, and he knew the Carlton attorneys could destroy the man's guardianship without taking the cap off one of their gold fountain pens, but Jennie didn't need any more stress in her life, and a confrontation between him and her friend would definitely cause her that.

"I know the garden is beautiful," she continued. "At least, I believe it is. But I also know that before long I will be able to tell anyone where each rock, bench and rose-bush is. Please, Edward. A walk is all I'm asking for. Just a short one?"

She thought he would refuse her. He saw disappointment in her tentative smile and heard it in her voice, and he knew that he was unable to deny her this as he had been unable to deny her anything else she had ever asked.

She had never asked, he realized. Except—except on occasion for something *for* him. But never for anything *from* him.

He lifted his hand to her cheek but dropped it when he felt her small start of surprise.

"A walk it is," he said, willing the tension from his body and from his voice. "To the center of the village?"

Her smile seemed to light her from within. "Oh, thank you, Edward. Is it far?"

Do I look as though I'm capable of knowing when I do or don't feel well...

Her words took on new meaning as Edward realized Jennie had no concept of the town outside the confines of the garden wall. Her doctor's office, perhaps. But that was near the new hospital, much too far for her to travel except by car. In all their loving concern for Jennie, had the people of this town kept her a virtual prisoner at the vicar's home?

"Edward?"

"No," he told her, hearing unspoken questions in her soft calling of his name. *Is it too far to walk? Have you changed your mind? Are you afraid I'm not strong enough? Do you not want to spend that much time with me?* "No, it's not far at all. And I think I saw a soda fountain on this side of Main Street. If you're really good, I might be persuaded to buy you a root beer.''

He wanted to call back his words before he had finished speaking. *If she were really good.* Damn! Even he sounded as though he thought she was a helpless child.

''Oh, that sounds wonderful,'' she said, laughing, either deliberately ignoring his words or accepting them as the teasing they once would have been. She stopped abruptly. ''I like root beer, don't I?''

He wanted to laugh with sheer enjoyment at the look of wonder on her face; he wanted to cry for the frustration she must feel. Instead, he turned her toward the gate and led her along the path. ''Jennie, you love root beer.''

She caught his arm, forcing him to stop and wait. Slowly, carefully, she raised her hand to his cheek, touching him lightly before drawing it back. ''Thank you.''

He needed her touch. More than the light caress of her fingers on his cheek. More than her gentle grasp on his arm. The thought appalled him. As a child, he had sworn never again to need anyone. When Jennie left him, he had repeated that vow. Twice now, someone had crept behind his defenses, trapping him in need. Twice now, that person had been Jennie.

Who was she that she could do this to him? Temptress and liar, or innocent victim? And would his need for her go away if he ever learned the truth? Somehow, he didn't think so. But that would be later, if ever. This was now, and his need demanded touch. Gently, he lifted her hand from his arm and placed it in his hand, entwining their fingers. ''You're welcome,'' he told her in response to her simple thanks, in response to the warmth that settled over and through him as her fingers clasped his. ''You're very welcome.''

Jennie felt the small shudder that ran through him as Edward laced his fingers with hers and guided her along the sidewalk that led to the heart of town. What emotion had prompted that reaction from him? Aversion? Need? She caught herself staring up at his face as though she could read his emotions. As though she could see. She broke off that thought before it had a chance to consume her. The darkness of the mood that would provoke was much worse than the darkness she lived with daily. It had come over her earlier that day and she had barely managed to escape it. She would not let it intrude on this time with Edward.

Edward. How right it seemed that she was with him, free in the sunlight. Yet, how strange it seemed, too.

Who was he?

Someone who had filled her life. She knew that. But not for long. She knew that, as well. She felt inexplicably, undeniably, drawn to him. But near the edge of that attraction, another shadow in her life of shadows, hovered the memory of a fear as great and as little understood as that which had claimed her that morning on the stairs. As that which sometimes woke her from her sleep.

She had left this man? Why? And had her fear come before or after she had left?

"Hello, Jennie."

"It's good to see you out, Jennie."

The two voices called out from a distance away, perhaps from across the street. Though they were friendly and familiar, it took her a moment to sort through her memories for their identity. When she found it, she smiled and waved.

She felt tension throb through Edward, then ease as he, too, recognized the casual friendliness of the two who were probably already hurrying away on whatever mission had brought them to the village.

"You knew them?" Edward asked.

Jennie nodded. "From church. Why? You sound surprised."

"Maybe a little," he admitted. "I was rapidly drawing a picture of you, locked away in the vicar's garden."

And maybe his picture wasn't quite so far off, she thought, but she chuckled. "At first, I think I may have been, but if so, I was the one closing the lock. It was just, oh—difficult, meeting people, not knowing if I was supposed to know them, not knowing how I appeared to them, not knowing—" She shrugged, trying to lighten her words and, maybe, succeeding. "Not knowing if I had dribbled food on my dress, or worse, would spill something on them."

He stopped and turned toward her on the sidewalk, halting her, and gripped her shoulders. "You could never be anything less than graceful, Jennie. Never."

He was hurting her. Not with his grasp, but somewhere deep inside, in a place hidden from her, as all her past was. But she wanted to believe his words, needed to believe his words. She drew a deep breath, bringing herself back to the reality of the sun-dappled sidewalk and Edward Carlton offering her such relentless tenderness.

Too much emotion. Too much. Instinctively, she withdrew from it and laughed lightly. "Thank you. But would you mind telling that to Caitlin? She might have a little trouble believing you, though, considering how often she had to clean up one of my spills."

His hands tightened on her shoulders, and she knew he was searching for words. She reached to cover one of his hands, giving it a little pat, then turned in the direction of the village. By simply linking her arm with his once again and starting to walk, she broke the too-serious mood.

"But you're right," she said. "I don't get out, except for church and the clinic, so this is all new to me."

"Then you need the tourist's special, don't you?"

She breathed a silent thanks when she realized that he had let her change to a less troubling subject. "Please."

Again he hesitated, searching, she knew. When he spoke his voice carried a slight strain, as though he'd rather cover much more important territory than describing terrain, but as he continued, the strain lessened.

"The sidewalk is brick," he said, "which I suppose you had already discovered."

She nodded and chuckled. That fact had been hard to miss with her sliding, almost hesitant, steps when they'd first started this walk.

"It's wide, and on the street side there are black street-lights that look like gas lamps, which are surrounded by raised brick planters full of spring flowers. On your right is a tall, black wrought-iron fence. I can't tell you what's behind it, because overgrown fir trees about a hundred feet back effectively block any view. But the verge between the fence and the row of trees is well trimmed, and there are beds of spring flowers.

"The street is brick, too," he continued. "Did you know that?"

"No. How unusual."

"Not for this town," he told her. "Most of them are. At least the ones close to the heart of the village."

"Village," she said. "That's not the first time you've used that term, is it?"

"No. And it probably won't be the last time, either. Jennie, if you could see this town, you would love it. You'd be reaching for your sketch pad and telling me it's like a Currier and Ives painting. And you'd ask where the snow was and why all the people on the streets were in modern dress instead of Victorian—"

He broke off his words abruptly and stopped on the sidewalk. Jennie paused beside him, silent for a moment, as she realized he had just inadvertently given her something very precious—a glimpse of the woman she had once been. A woman who took pleasure from the simple act of living. A woman who saw beauty in brick sidewalks and spring flowers and quaint buildings. A woman to whom vision—oh, God, a woman to whom vision was as important as life.

Was that why she didn't remember? Was facing a world of shadow too horrible to bear if the memories of sight were also there? Or was there another reason? Was facing a life without the man who now stood silently beside her too horrible to bear if the memories of loving him were also there?

"I would?" she asked.

His voice sounded suspiciously hoarse as he laced his fingers with hers and resumed their stroll. "You would," he said.

Six

A hush fell over the soda shop as Edward opened the door and ushered her in. Jennie paused, unsure of herself, as she so often was, until he urged her forward with a gentle touch on her hand.

"They look friendly enough," he told her in a whisper as the conversations resumed around them. "Young, but probably not hostile."

She turned her head sharply in his direction. "Who?"

"The natives. It looks like we've found the after-school crowd. Look—sorry," he said, and she was close enough to feel his shoulders shrug. "There's the sheriff's daughter—Jamie?—waving at us."

"Where?"

"To your right and about twenty feet away."

Jennie smiled in the direction he indicated and gave a friendly wave. "Anyone else?" she asked.

"I don't know who you know, but most of them just seem mildly curious. About me," he added as she felt herself begin to tense. "Here we are." She heard the light scrape of a chair against the floor and then the equally light pressure of Edward's hands on her shoulders as he guided her to the seat.

"Two root beers," she heard him say as he helped her scoot closer to the table. "Do you want anything else? Ice cream? A sandwich?"

Either he had forgotten her earlier fears about eating with him already, which seemed unlikely, or he was ignoring them, trusting her not to make a fool of both of them. Nevertheless, she wouldn't risk it. She shook her head and rested her hands on what felt like a circular, marble table-top.

"Okay. That will be all, then."

He was giving the order already? Apparently he was. She heard the scrape of his chair as he seated himself close beside her and resumed his running commentary on the sights around them, letting her *see* with his eyes and his perception.

"It looks as though this place was last redecorated about 1925," he said, "and kept in remarkably good repair ever since. The floor is covered with tiny white tiles, and the walls with larger white ones, accented with squares of dark green. The tables are green marble, and the chairs are black—iron, I think, with the same stylized Art Deco arches and lines I saw at the airport. The soda fountain—"

His description blended with the sounds and aromas of the room around them—eager conversations muted by the music now coming from the jukebox, loud enough for young ears but not intrusively so, hamburgers and French fries cooking, and the soft brush of air stirred by ceiling fans.

"Here you are." A young voice interrupted Jennie's reverie as the waitress set glasses on the table. "I hope you enjoy this, Jennie. We're really glad to see you out and about. Oh, and these are on the house. Let me know if you need anything else.''

She was gone before Jennie had time to thank her, or to identify the woman's voice.

''Amazing,'' she heard Edward say beside her. ''This town and the people in it have yet to fail to amaze me.''

''Are they really so special, or am I reading too much into the kindness with which I've been treated?''

''I don't know.'' She heard perplexity in his voice. ''I've never encountered anything like it. I want to say that most of what I've found is an act. But for what reason? So I...I just don't know.''

Perplexity. And suspicion. What had happened to Edward to cause him to doubt kindness? Was it what she had done? Or something that had happened before her? Something that might explain why she had—had *what? What had she done?*

She reached for her drink and found it in a chilled glass mug. Frosty cold, just the way...just the way she liked it. Now, why on earth could she suddenly remember something that inane and not even know with certainty that her name really was what she had been told?

''Will you tell me how we met?''

For a moment, he remained so silent, so still, she thought he wasn't going to answer her. She lifted the mug to her lips and sipped her drink, trying to pretend that it wasn't important if he didn't tell her.

''I ran you down.''

''What?''

''I literally tripped over you,'' he told her. ''At the marina.'' He sighed and hesitated again before proceeding. ''My father's boat had been sold years before. I had managed to locate it, and finally I had been able to buy it back. I was at the marina to take possession of it after years of believing it was gone forever. I wasn't paying attention to anything but the *Lady B,* and I crashed into you, sending you sprawling.

"I don't know how I could have missed you, though. You were wearing a pair of old, soft purple denims with colorful paint splatters all over them, an orange sweatshirt, and you had your hair tied back with a bright red bandanna.

"I thought you were a homeless person, at first, until I noticed that everything about you, especially your glorious hair, was squeaky clean, and that the parcel I'd knocked out of your hands was really a portfolio, a neon green portfolio, that had fallen open to reveal an exquisite sketch of the *Lady B.*"

"So you picked me up, dusted me off and—and what?"

"Not quite." He laughed softly, ruefully. "I demanded to know why you were sketching that particular boat, and you looked up at me, and down your nose at the same time—a real trick—and said 'People don't usually complain about what I choose to sketch.' Then *you* picked yourself up, dusted yourself off and took your portfolio out of my hands."

"Oh, dear."

"And that's when I noticed that in the fall you'd scraped your hands, as well as ripped one knee of those disreputable purple jeans, and my conscience kicked in. I was convinced that you had planted yourself in my way, with that sketch, in some devious plot to meet me... I'm afraid I told you as much, later, but right then I only knew I had to offer you at least minimal first aid, so I invited you on board the *Lady B.* And you said, 'I don't think we ought to do that. There doesn't seem to be a crew, or anyone to give us permission to board.'"

The scene unfolded before her eyes, not memory, but a film in living color and wraparound sound made possible by Edward's words.

"It was days before I truly believed you hadn't engineered our meeting, and weeks before I believed you didn't know who I was."

"Edward?" She groped across the table until she found his hand. "Who are you?"

She felt him tense.

"Just a man, Jennie. One who once thought he had reason to doubt the motives of anyone and everyone he met."

"And do you still?" she asked softly.

His hand turned and grasped hers. "Sometimes," he admitted. "Yes. Sometimes I still do."

Even after his admission, even after Jennie realized she might always be one of those persons he doubted, she found their walk home pleasant. Rather than tucking her hand in the crook of his arm, he held her hand, guiding her with soft words and gentle pressure while he continued his perceptive descriptions of the town, of the people they met along the walk, and, perhaps not knowing it, of himself.

Although tired when they reached the front gate of the vicarage garden, Jennie was reluctant to enter the house. Reluctant to leave Edward, she admitted to herself, this strange, reserved and yet giving man. And perhaps he was reluctant to leave her. He slowed his steps as they neared the door, then he dropped her hand and draped his arm around her shoulder, turning her toward the garden.

Totally lost after the first few turns, she let him lead her quietly into the cool, shaded depths of an area she had just hours before thought she knew as well as the interior of the room she had called home for the past six months.

She felt the ground beneath her feet change as they stepped from the brick onto a smooth, grassy area, where the air was redolent of the aroma of a flowering shrub unknown to Jennie but which grew in only one place in the garden. He had brought her to the bench where she had been sitting the day he arrived. The one from which she had begun the journey that had landed her ignominiously at his feet.

He didn't release her. Instead, he turned her until she faced him in the secluded glen and stood silently, with his hands on her shoulders echoing the tension she felt emanating from him.

No. More than just a reluctance to leave her had led him to bring her here. More than just a reluctance to leave her kept him silent, while he studied her with an intensity she could feel.

"Who are you, Jennie?" he asked softly, rephrasing her earlier question to him as he drew her closer.

She stared up at him, as lost in her emotions as she was in her darkness, as lost as she'd been when they'd first entered the garden. Would he kiss her? Was that where this was leading? They were married; surely they had been intimate. Her body was telling her they had been, demanding that she lean closer, that she feel the solid strength of him against her softness, that she take for herself a place with this man that she could not remember ever knowing—a place that was uniquely hers, and yet was shared with—with...with what? With someone who had every reason to doubt her, perhaps even to hate her.

"I was hoping..." Her throat tightened, choking off her softly spoken words. "I was hoping," she repeated, "that you could tell me."

Closer still he drew her, until she felt his breath like soft whispers across her cheek as he spoke. "Once I thought I knew. But did I, Jennie? Did I ever really know who you are?"

His strange question swirled through her darkness. But was it so strange? Had he known her? Had anyone ever really known her? Had anyone ever really wanted to know her?

His hands tightened on her upper arms with almost painful intensity. His breath, now hot, now harsh, fanned her cheek. "Damn it," he said, and the words seemed drawn from him as much against his will as the embrace that drew her to him. "What are you doing to me? What am I letting you do to me?"

She couldn't have answered, even if she had known how. His mouth claimed hers, silencing her brief, startled exclamation. No, in spite of his actions of the past few hours, this man she had married and then left was not a gentle man. She felt a tightly restrained anger simmering through him, a frustration and a hunger, perhaps—probably—unwanted. But he was not a violent man, either. She found no pain from his touch. Only a longing for something... something...

This was not the way it was supposed to be, Jennie knew. Not reluctant, not furtive, not... not...

And then she lost all thought of how their being together was supposed to be in the emotions that swamped her. "Yes," she whispered against his lips, giving voice to the rightness of being in this man's arms—again—to the rightness of lifting her hands to his shoulders and drawing him closer, to the rightness of surrendering to the hunger and desire she felt growing within herself.

"Jenn-nn-ie? Oh, Jenn-nn-ie? Where are you?"

She felt Edward's hands clench on her shoulders as Jamie's musical call rang through the garden. "Saved by your sheriff," he muttered as he stepped back from her.

"Oh, hi!" Jamie's words, breathless and sounding a little surprised, came from only a few feet away.

Jennie drew her errant nerves together as she emotionally and physically took one step back from Edward, unsure of what she had just experienced, unsure of how Edward would react to her uninhibited response to a desire he so clearly resented. "Hello, yourself," she said to Jamie, wondering at the girl's surprise. Jamie had known she was with Edward. Not half an hour earlier, Jamie had stopped by their table as she left the soda shop. ''Is something wrong?''

''No. Well, not really. Mrs. Higgins was wondering where you were, and *Dad* wants to talk to *you*, Mr. Carlton.''

''Now, why doesn't that surprise me?'' Edward replied as Jennie felt his arm drape around her shoulder in a gesture that could only be proprietary although she doubted that anyone other than she would know the tension that still gripped him. Tension, not necessarily desire. ''Tell Mrs. Higgins and your father that we'll be with them in a few minutes.''

''Yeah, well...'' At a loss for words for the first time since Jennie had met her, Jamie hesitated and stammered slightly. ''It's just that Dad says you've got a long-distance call, Mr. Carlton, maybe a pretty important one, from someone named Slater?''

''Damn!''

''Edward? What's wrong?''

''Nothing,'' he said, even as he began withdrawing from her. ''Nothing,'' he said again. ''You'll see that Jennie gets back to the house all right?''

''Well, of course,'' Jamie said.

''Edward?''

''Later, Jennie,'' he said, distracted and much farther distanced from her than the scant two feet separating them. ''We'll talk. Later.''

She felt a wall between them, as real as a physical one, yet neither it nor Edward's withdrawal brought her any real surprise. Had she experienced it before? With him? Or with...with whom?

''Will we?'' she asked quietly.

She felt his hand gentle on her cheek, and for a moment the wall was gone. ''Yes. Oh, yes. Count on it, Jennie.''

Then, as he drew his hand from her, he seemed to wrap himself back in his isolation. The faint sound of his footsteps on the brick walk only emphasized what Jennie already knew. He was gone. But deep inside herself, she knew that he had left her before he walked away.

Lambert was waiting for him by the front gate.

"Where can I take the call?" Edward asked.

Lambert nodded toward his Land Rover parked at the curb. "I told him I'd have you at my office when he called back."

"And you just happened to know that the call was important enough to search for me and disturb my visit with Jennie?"

Lambert nodded once, slightly, acknowledging Edward's sarcasm and his anger. "I've known where you were since you left the lodge this morning. And yes, I recognized Paul Slater's name. I'm a competent investigator, Carlton, even though you might not think so. But I'm also sensible enough to accept help from any other competent source, and Paul Slater is extremely competent.

"Something else you might not believe is that I do want what is best for Jennie. If that happens to be you, fine. But if I find out it isn't, there's no way in hell I'll let you take her outside of these garden walls ever again."

Edward met the sheriff's steady appraisal with one of his own. Only the knowledge that he at last believed this man kept him from unleashing on him all the power of the Carlton empire. "That's fair enough," he said. "Let's go take that telephone call."

The telephone rang only minutes after they arrived in Lambert's office. The sheriff handed Edward the phone and then, in an act of courtesy that surprised Edward, stood to leave the room.

Edward wanted privacy for the call, privacy to learn the secrets Slater had unearthed about Jennie's past, but he knew those secrets might have a bearing on what had happened to her, and if so, he would only have to repeat the conversation to the sheriff.

He shook his head as he took the receiver. "You don't have to leave."

Lambert raised an eyebrow but seated himself behind the desk with what a casual observer would have thought lazy indifference.

"Paul," Edward said to the man on the phone. "I'm glad you called. I had planned to talk with you after I received your report. But if you can just sketch in the highlights now, maybe we won't need to talk again after I read it."

"Yeah. Well..." For the first time since he'd met met him, Edward heard indecision in Paul Slater's voice. "Madeline said something about a file mix-up?"

"You might call it that. Our file was empty when she went to retrieve your report."

"So was mine."

"*What?*"

Lambert glanced up sharply. With a gesture, he indicated a speaker attachment to the telephone console.

"Hang on a minute, Paul." Edward studied what Slater had just said. Coincidence? Not likely, even not considering what had happened to Jennie. But with those events factored in? No. No coincidence. "I'm going to let the sheriff in on the rest of this conversation."

Lambert nodded and punched in the command.

"Now," Edward said. "*Your* file was empty, too?"

"That's right. Hard copy, and when I checked the computer, I found that that one was, too. Oh, the files were there. There just wasn't anything in them."

"How long has it been since you last saw the report?" Lambert asked.

"Not since I delivered it."

"Before the wedding?" Edward asked.

"Oh, yeah. Quite a bit before. According to last year's calendar and the billing, mid-October. You didn't see it?"

Edward glanced up to see Lambert studying him with a slow, measuring glance. "No."

"Mr. Slater, is there any chance you can reconstruct this report?" the sheriff asked.

"Sure. It might take a day or so, but I remember the investigation fairly well because it turned out to be so much different from what I expected when I first started it. And that's why I was so surprised when things didn't work out between the two of you. This doesn't have anything to do with divorce proceedings, does it, Edward? Because I can assure you there's nothing in what I found to help Fallon with any kind of case."

"Not even the disgruntled professor, or the reasons for the abandoned adoption and all those moves?" Edward said.

For a moment, silence filled the room. Then Paul coughed once, as though covering a laugh. "It appears to me that you paid a lot of money for a report that nobody in your office read. Those were preliminary comments to Madeline which, in light of what I later discovered, I wish I'd never made."

"You discussed this with Ms. Harrison?" Lambert asked, but now his soft voice carried the tone of interrogation.

"Sheriff, for all practical purposes, she was my client. Yes, I gave her several preliminary reports before I submitted the final written one. Which apparently she didn't read, either."

"That was just a comment, Mr. Slater, not an accusation," Lambert said in the slow, gravelly voice that no longer deceived Edward. The man was as sharp as any big-city cop, maybe sharper. "But what we're looking at here is a lot more serious than grounds for divorce.

"Mrs. Carlton was the victim of—well, we're not sure just of what. What we're looking for in your report is anything that might help us with our investigation."

"My God. She's not dead, is she?"

"No," Edward told him. "She just—she just doesn't remember—"

"She doesn't remember how she got from San Francisco to Avalon," Lambert said, interrupting easily but firmly. "Or how she got to be pretty seriously injured. Do you suppose there's anything in what you know that could help us?"

"No... No. Good Lord, the woman's led such a squeaky-clean life, I had a hard time convincing myself it wasn't some sort of made-up identity."

"And it wasn't?" Edward asked.

"I'd stake my license on it, Edward. Look, my notebooks are in storage, but if I get on this right away, I can reconstruct the report and get it out to you—tomorrow? The day after? Is that okay? I can fax it—"

"No," Edward said. The fewer eyes who saw this, the better.

"Right," Paul continued. "I'll courier it out as soon as I finish."

"Thanks, Paul."

"Where do you want it sent?"

"Why don't you send it to Mr. Carlton in care of my office," Lambert said. "And Mr. Slater," he added, almost as an afterthought, "who has had access to your files and computer?"

"That's a damned good question, Sheriff. One I guess I thought I knew the answer to. Let me do a little checking, and I'll send you a separate report covering that."

"Why don't you telephone me instead? I want to do some checking of my own, but I might have a few things you can help me with. How is your schedule? Would you have time to spend a few days on this?"

"For Edward. Yes, of course. How is—how is Mrs. Carlton?"

"She's—" Edward began, before Lambert interrupted. "She is recovering nicely, Mr. Slater. Quite nicely."

"She's recovering quite nicely?" Edward said as he leaned back in the chair.

Lambert nodded at him across the desk. "Your file on Jennie was missing and you didn't consider it worthy of a comment to me?"

"Not really. I thought its disappearance strange, maybe, but I did not consider it ominous until Paul called. And since I didn't even know about the file until a few hours ago—"

"Is it normal for your administrative assistant to investigate your personal relationships? To act on her own without consulting you about either the investigation or the results?"

Edward shook his head. "Madeline Harrison is more than an administrative assistant, Sheriff. She's a good friend, a member of the family and a valued employee. She doesn't know it yet, but plans are already under way to promote her to a vice presidency."

"Do you have any idea when the file might have been taken?"

Edward paused. In light of what Paul had just told them, he could no longer believe it was simply missing. "My office was broken into the day of my wedding. That's why I left Jennie alone at the apartment."

"What else was taken?"

"From the office? Nothing. Apparently, whoever got in was surprised by security soon after entry."

"Or had gotten the only thing wanted."

"But why?" Edward asked. "If we trust Paul's evaluation, there was nothing in the report that was damaging. And when were Paul's files disturbed?"

"Where are Mr. Slater's offices?" Lambert asked. "In the same building as yours?"

Edward shook his head. "We've talked about moving him in, because we use his firm's services so often, but no. He's halfway across town."

"Interesting," Lambert said. "Interesting." He pulled a small notebook from an inner pocket of his suit jacket. "Three men arrived with Ms. Harrison—Tim Huxton, Wiley Phelps and George Daniels. How well do you know them?"

And so it began once more. The nightmare he had sworn he would never let himself be vulnerable to again. "Anyone and everyone, right? No one is safe from suspicion. Everyone's motives are suspect."

"I'm sorry, Mr. Carlton. I can only imagine how difficult this is for you. But there is a difference this time. We have Jennie. She is safe."

"Yes. Safe in a world of darkness. Safe in a world with no memories. Tell me, Sheriff, how would you feel if you were *safe* the way she is?"

"I'd hate it like hell, just as I imagine Jennie does."

Edward saw again the image of Jennie as she had fallen on the path in front of him that first day, her eyes filled with tears, her small fists flailing at the brick walk in frustration. "Yes. I imagine she does."

"I know you're running a business," Lambert said, calling Edward back to the reality of the sheriff's office, "but I'd appreciate it if you'd give me notice of anyone else who will be coming to Avalon." He took his gold pen from his pocket and held it poised over his notebook. "Now, let's go over the backgrounds of the employees who arrived today."

"Do you really think Jennie is in danger from any of my employees?"

"Do you know who harmed your wife, Mr. Carlton?"

"No."

"Do you know why?"

Why? None of his earlier beliefs fit the woman he had met here in Avalon any more than they fit the woman he had knocked from her feet at the marina almost a year ago. "No."

Lambert smiled grimly. "Then humor me. The sooner we go over this, the sooner you can get back to Jennie. That is where you want to go when you leave here, isn't it?"

It was, and it wasn't. "Tim Huxton has been in charge of setting up temporary field offices for Carlton Enterprises for the last ten years. At the moment, he's looking for offices for a fairly large administrative staff to relocate here and stay for as long as I believe necessary. He's also looking for a place for me to live. When I have a house instead of a room at the lodge, are you going to object to my moving Jennie out of Reverend Winthrop's—custody?"

"I don't know, Carlton." Lambert placed his pen beside his notebook and met Edward's scrutiny. "When you have a house instead of a room at the lodge, are you going to insist on moving Jennie out of Reverend Winthrop's—safekeeping?"

Lambert knew him too well. Knew the betrayal he felt that wouldn't let him forget the way Jennie had left. Knew the doubts that still plagued him about the future. Knew that Edward would not force Jennie to leave the safety she had found until he had resolved those doubts. One way or the other.

Edward glanced at the notebook on the desk. "Wiley Phelps is my pilot," he said. "I hired him right after I assumed control of the company. He's a former air-force officer with an impeccable background. George Daniels has only been with us about five years. Tim hired him while George was still in graduate school. Paul Slater ran the background check."

Grimly, remembering another time when he had gone through this drill, Edward carefully and completely briefed

the sheriff on each member of the crew that had arrived in Avalon.

This time was different, he told himself. Jennie was safe. Not like—not like his parents. Not like Meggie. Sweet little Meggie with her huge dark eyes all filled with tears as she had begged him to go with them that day. She hadn't understood why he was being punished, hadn't understood why their father wouldn't let him go with them. Twenty-five years had passed since he had promised his little sister he would see her the next day, and *he* still didn't understand why he hadn't been with them. Still hadn't forgotten the fear or the pain or the grief.

Yes, this time was different. Jennie had left him. She hadn't been taken. No one would contact him with a demand for money in exchange for her life. He would not have to endure the weeks of waiting as he had until his parents' bodies were found in an abandoned boathouse on a wild and isolated stretch of northern California beach, the further weeks while the police searched for Meggie's body but never found it.

But if this time was so different, why were his fear and his pain and grief so much the same?

"Mr. Carlton?" The sheriff's soft, gravelly voice once again called him back to the present. "Are you all right?"

Edward sighed. "Ghosts, Sheriff. Maybe I shouldn't admit to them, but then, you already know about my ghosts, don't you?"

"Yes," Lambert admitted. "Yes."

Edward stood, in an effort to shake off the memories. "Is there anything else you need to know? If so, let's get it over with." He looked around. As luxurious as it was, Lambert's office was a reminder of other offices, other cops. "I want to get out of here. I want to get out of here now."

Seven

Jennie was laughing at something Reverend Winthrop must have just said to her when Caitlin showed Edward into the dining room the next morning. In the long hours of his sleepless night, he'd wondered if he'd ever forget how laughter lighted her eyes and curved her lovely lips. He'd wondered if he'd ever forget the taste of her, the touch of her now that he had once again held her in his arms. But he hadn't known until just that moment how empty he had been without her soft, musical laughter to soften the harsh edges of his life.

Her laughter faded with the first sound of his footsteps on the polished hardwood dining room floor, reminding him of all their unresolved problems.

He saw her head tilt slightly as she listened, attempting to identify who had entered the room.

"Good morning," he said, identifying himself by his voice for her benefit.

"Good morning, Mr. Carlton." Mrs. Winthrop smiled and indicated a chair across the table from Jennie, apparently not at all surprised by the arrival of an unexpected guest at her table. "I'm so glad you could join us for breakfast this morning."

Edward watched as Jennie squared her shoulders and folded her hands in her lap. Remembering her telling him of her embarrassment about her various spills while eating, he returned Mrs. Winthrop's smile but did not walk farther into the room. "Thank you, but I haven't come to intrude on your breakfast. I have an appointment with your husband. Apparently, I'm early." He turned toward the minister. "Perhaps I should return later?"

Reverend Winthrop placed his napkin beside his plate and stood. "Nonsense, my boy. I've finished." He glanced toward Caitlin. "Please bring us some coffee."

There were many things Edward felt he had to discuss with the man who had housed and fed and clothed his wife—Edward's financial responsibility being only one of them, but they had been seated in the front parlor with the coffee the minister had insisted upon for only a few moments, far too little time even to begin to explore the morass of confused responsibilities and allegiances and needs, when a soft knock sounded at the doorway and Jennie stepped into the room.

"Am I wrong in thinking this discussion is about me?" she asked.

Edward glanced from her to the minister with an unvoiced question, but Winthrop only returned the questioning glance.

"No, you're not wrong," Edward told her.

"Then shouldn't I be present?" she asked, obviously not sure she would be invited to stay.

How do I look? Do I look competent? Do I look as though I'm not capable of knowing . . .

Yes. He was treating her as everyone else had been treating her for the past months, and no matter how they finally resolved the problems between them, this was not fair—to her, or even to himself.

"Perhaps you should."

He saw the tension leave her shoulders. With a grace he admired and knew few could duplicate, she made her way across the room to the mantel, where she turned and faced the room. "Reverend Winthrop?"

"I'm here, Jennie," the minister told her from his place in the wing chair facing the one in which Edward sat.

She nodded, pinpointing his location. "Thank you," she said, then fell silent.

Waiting? For them to continue their conversation? For him to notice how the painting behind her framed and emphasized her delicate coloring and fine features? How the painting behind called forth, for him, all the pain and anger of the past six months, and all the indecision he now faced?

"Here," Edward said, rising abruptly. "Take this chair."

Jennie shook her head. "No, thank you. I'd rather stand."

Well, hell. What did he do now? Insist she sit? Insist she move away from the painting? And then what? Explain why he couldn't bear to look at her standing there?

He paced to the front windows and turned. From that position, he could see her, but not the painting, and he could maintain eye contact with the minister.

"Edward?"

"I'm here, Jennie."

"Yes, I know," she said softly. "Standing by the window. Worrying? About what? I wonder."

She amazed him, as much now as in the first magical weeks after they met. He'd never been able to refuse anything she'd asked of him. Could he now? Even when telling her might—probably would—bring her unnecessary pain?

"Jennie." Miraculously, Reverend Winthrop broke the silence, rescuing Edward from the cautious answer he had begun formulating. "Dr. Freede, Sheriff Lambert and I all agree that spending time with Mr. Carlton can only be beneficial for you, in the long run. But we are aware that— that at this moment—you have no memory of your prior relationship. We have no desire to cause you undue stress—"

"But would I mind spending more time—a great deal more time?—with the man who tells me he is my husband?" Jennie finished his question for him in the same soft voice with which she had asked her own.

Winthrop sighed, and Edward released the breath he had not realized he'd been holding.

"Exactly, my dear," the minister said.

Would she? Edward watched her expressive features as Jennie questioned herself silently. A tiny frown creased her forehead as she tilted her head and looked toward where he stood. And if she did mind, if she refused to spend more time with him after the passionate way he had touched her the day before, what would he do? And why—*why?*—did he feel as though she held his future in her small, talented hands?

"No," she said finally. "No, I won't mind. The real question, though, is not will I mind, but will Edward?"

"Do you mind?" Jennie asked later as Edward guided her along the path toward his rented Jeep. "You never did say."

She fought the unreasoning disappointment his lack of answer to her question had caused her, knowing that not answering was in itself an answer. He had to be remembering yesterday, his unwanted lack of control. And hers. Of course he minded. And then she fought an unreasoning sense of having felt that same disappointment many times. Because of Edward? Was that why she had left him? Or was this knowledge of disappointment much older, much deeper than the marriage she couldn't remember?

He was radiating as much tension as she felt.

"*Do* you mind?" she asked again.

He stopped and turned, blocking her forward movement. For a moment, she thought he might touch her, but instead he held himself rigidly still. Even his arm beneath her hand felt like stone. "Edward?"

"Drop it, Jennie."

His voice wasn't particularly loud and it wasn't particularly harsh, but in it she heard an inherent authority, once which tolerated no defiance.

Drop it, she heard again, if only in her mind. *Back off. Let it go.* She'd heard those words before. Often? Too often? But from him?

Humor. If she could find something light to say, a joke to make, a way to coax him to laughter, she could avoid . . . avoid . . . avoid what? Avoid pushing him headlong into anger? No. No, she realized with an insight she had no way of knowing she had felt before—she needed to avoid revealing just how much being pushed away hurt. Had always hurt.

But instead of the humor she needed, when she searched within herself, she found a sudden image of a little girl—herself?—standing beside an older woman, one she was sure she didn't know, at least not well, outside a large brick building. A hospital? And the woman saying, "You'll have to go back. There's no other way. My daughter is too fragile to care for you now. She can't look at you and not remember the plans she'd made."

"Jennie?"

The concern in Edward's voice drew her forward in time. She looked up, cursing the shadows that would not let her see his face, his eyes.

"What's wrong?"

No. She'd found no humor, nothing light to coax him into laughter. She'd found—what? "A memory, I think," she told him. "But an old one, a very old one. And I don't know if it's really mine or only something I once read or saw."

She lifted her free hand to his arm, needing to anchor herself to his solid strength. "Did I tell you about my childhood?"

"No."

Their marriage had lasted only hours, but surely they'd had some common bond on which to base it. Hadn't they?

"Did you tell me about yours?"

"Yes."

Yes. Just that one word. And the wall slammed back around him, keeping her at a distance.

"Did I—did I betray a trust? Did I somehow twist that knowledge—"

"Jennie—"

The pain in his voice silenced her. Somehow, she knew this man didn't often let his emotions show. Unable to stop herself, she lifted her hand to his face. He flinched slightly at her first touch but did not move away from her as she traced her fingers along his jaw, finding it both strong and obstinate. A noisy car rattled down the nearby street. Reluctantly, she drew her hand from his face and turned toward the street, lifting her own obstinate jaw but giving him a rueful smile. "We're going to have a problem getting to know each other unless we find something we can talk about, Edward."

He sighed, lifted her hand to his arm and began walking toward the street. "I know."

"What did we do together when we were—we did...date, didn't we?"

Edward chuckled, the light laugh sounding less forced than his words. "Yes, we dated."

"And we went places together?"

He covered her hand with his and squeezed lightly. "We went to galleries and antique shops, for walks along the beach, and sailing on the *Lady B.*"

"Oh." Damn! She wanted to scream. Had everything been taken from her? "Well, scratch those," she said instead. "Was there anything I particularly liked to do—or you? What did you do before we—before we met?"

"Before you, Jennie, I worked. A twelve-hour day was not uncommon, an eighteen-hour day not unheard of."

She heard the formality creeping back into his voice. "Oh, dear. We'd better scratch that, too," she said, striving for a word, a laugh, anything to lighten his mood but not finding it. Edward had been somber when they began this outing. If he became any more formal, any more tense, he'd be like one of the small concrete statues scattered through the garden more than the warm, giving man she had glimpsed during the days since he'd arrived in Avalon.

"What do you have planned for us today?" she asked lightly.

"You're sure I have something planned?"

She laughed. "Edward, I can't imagine you tolerating much unstructured time. In fact, I suspect the last few days have been driving you slightly mad."

His hand spasmed on hers, and she realized that he could have interpreted her words in more than one way.

"You might say that," he told her, and his words were as light as hers, much lighter than his posture and the touch of his hand on hers revealed.

She felt the kiss of a shadow on her face and then sunlight, signaling that they had reached the sidewalk outside the garden.

"I'm parked over here," he said, turning slightly.

"So you do have something planned."

She waited through the awkward shuffle while he released her hand, opened the car door for her and helped her off the curb. "It's a little higher than a conventional car. How can I help you?"

As much as she resented needing any help, she appreciated that he had offered, not just attempted to stuff her into the vehicle. "Give me a moment," she said. "Please."

Yes, the vehicle was taller than the vicar's comfortable sedan, but not a great deal. And it was completely out of keeping with the image she had formed of Edward and the type of vehicle he would choose. She ran her hand up around the door facing, finding its height, and then down to pat the softly upholstered seat. No, she discovered, there was no graceful way for her to fumble her way in.

"This isn't so bad," she said, offering Edward a smile as she turned her back to the car and eased her upper body through the door and then raised on her toes to perch against the seat with the lip of the frame just touching the backs of her knees.

She heard his reluctant chuckle, a barren, lingering silence, and then felt his hands as he finished the job of lifting her into the seat and turning her.

"There," he said, sounding slightly breathless. "There."

The door closed with a solid thud, leaving her alone in the interior of the car, her legs and waist still tingling from the touch of his hands on them, her heart and lungs racing with her unexpected physical reaction. He'd been touching her all morning, for cripes' sakes, so why, suddenly, had her entire system gone on overload? *Because until just that moment, he had been guiding a blind woman, nothing more.*

Jennie leaned her head back against the padded rest and closed her eyes. And when he'd helped her into the car, he'd simply been helping a blind woman. Nothing more. But why, then, had it felt like so much more. Why then had it seemed as though he, too, felt the jolt of awareness that had rocked her when he lifted her.

Another door opened, and she heard Edward settle into the seat. She turned toward him and her hand struck some sort of console separating them.

"I'm sorry," he said. "I should have traded vehicles with Madeline. I didn't think about how awkward this one would be for you."

Madeline. Madeline? Why did that name sound so impossibly familiar? Jennie tucked it away to ask about later. Right now she had to tend to something else. "No more awkward than Reverend Winthrop's car the first time I rode in it, or Sheriff Lambert's. This one is fine, Edward." She ran her hand over the slightly nubby upholstery. "It smells new."

"It's a rental, Jennie. I didn't know what kind of terrain I'd be driving into."

"Oh. Well, it is comfortable."

"Sure it is. Tell me, do you ever complain about anything? Ever lose your temper or that damn, calm acceptance of yours?"

His harshly spoken attack stilled her restless hand on the upholstery and kept her silent and wondering just what she had done to bring it on, wondering why it seemed all the more violent because he didn't raise his voice above the level with which he had spoken to Mrs. Winthrop, to Jamie or to her in what she had thought softer moments.

Not fair! Not when she had tried so hard to hide her darker thoughts and emotions. Not when she'd believed she was doing so well.

"You know better than that," she said finally. "I fell apart, practically at your feet, the day you arrived. My God, only yesterday I fainted and was put to bed like a sick child."

"Yes," he said with a controlled expulsion of breath. "Yes, of course, you're right."

She heard a soft, rustling sound and felt a slight shifting of weight as he turned, felt his hand hover over hers, touch it and then withdraw, leaving her alone in her darkness even though he sat only inches from her.

"I don't know how to deal with this, Jennie. I don't know how you do."

What a strange thing to say. "I deal with it because I have no choice, Edward."

This time when he brushed his hand over hers, he allowed it to linger, then to clasp her fingers. "I always suspected you were a stronger person than I am."

Jennie turned her hand and laced her fingers with his. A lifeline in the darkness. A respite from her isolation. She felt the pressure of too many unshed tears behind her eyes and clogging her throat. "Impossible," she told him. "I wouldn't feel so safe with you if that were true."

They sat there for a minute, then two, each wrapped in silence, but Jennie did not feel alone. When Edward tightened his fingers on hers, sighed and then slid his hand from hers, she almost knew what his next words would be.

"Maybe we are making some progress in this insane situation after all."

"Yes," she said. "Maybe we are." She turned in her seat to face the windshield, reluctant to give up the comfort of their moment but knowing they must go on. "What would you have been doing today if you hadn't come for me? It isn't the same thing you had planned for our outing, is it?"

"No," he admitted. "But maybe it should be." He sighed again and started the car. "Tim Huxton, my locations manager, has been here less than twenty-four hours and he already has some places located. I really need to make a decision on office space and on a place to live before I drive my crew to revolt."

"But you weren't going to take me house hunting."

"No."

Why? Because of their history? Or because she would be so useless, or perhaps because she would be so frustrated, with her lack of vision? "You know that nothing's going to be easy for us, don't you?" she asked quietly. "And that nothing I do where I can be seen by people I can't see is going to be particularly comfortable for me? We might as well do something—something *obviously* productive."

Tim had provided Edward with keys and three addresses—two office buildings and one house. The office locations were outside of town, past the airport in a relatively new subdivision, and Edward elected to view those first. Although he didn't ask for her input, he did describe each space as they walked through it. Even sightless, Jennie found them both luxurious and without charm, an effect she suspected must be extremely difficult to achieve in this quaint village. Apparently, Edward did, too.

"Amazing," he said softly as he helped her back into the car after leaving the second one, "I didn't think there was any place in this town that was fully in the twentieth century, but in less than a day, Tim's managed to find not one, but two places that, once one is past the outside walls, are interchangeable with countless offices in countless cities."

"Of all the gin joints in all the towns in all the world," Jennie said, not knowing where the words came from, just that they seemed to fit Edward's mood as much as his had.

When he didn't immediately close the door, she turned toward him.

"Casablanca," he said.

"What?"

"You just quoted a line from a movie."

Jennie fought back a frustrated moan. *Amazing?* Edward thought these offices were amazing. No. What was amazing was that she could remember that she liked root beer in frosty glass mugs and could quote film dialogue when she couldn't remember anything else about her life, even being married, being *intimate* with this man whose touch had become so essential to her.

He touched his hand to her cheek. "You wore out your second copy of the videotape right after I met you," he told her. He couldn't read her mind, that much she did know, but his words made her wonder, just for a moment.

She caught his hand with hers and held it tightly before nodding abruptly. "I liked this film, did I?"

"You might say that. You once told me that spending an evening with a bowl of popcorn, a bottle of root beer, a box of tissues and that movie was better than going to most gallery showings. Of course, you didn't cry at gallery showings."

"And I did when I watched this film?"

"Every time," he said. Slowly, almost reluctantly, he withdrew his hand from hers. "I think those were the only times I ever saw you cry."

The door slammed with a solid thud, leaving Jennie with questions she wasn't sure she was brave enough to want to know the answers to. *But she was brave enough not to let him know how scared she was.*

She heard Edward's door open and felt the slight shift of weight as he settled into the seat. "You have another location to check out?" she asked when he only sat there, not closing his door, not starting the engine.

"What? Oh. Oh, yes. A house. Although after what we've seen, and with it at the bottom of Tim's list of possibilities, I'm almost afraid to. Do you feel up to it?"

Did she? If she were honest with him, she'd admit that what she really wanted to do was hide in her room alone. No. If she were completely honest with herself, she'd admit that what she really wanted to do was hide in a room with him to hold her and hold the world at bay. With him to—to—

"Yes," she said, straightening her shoulders and reaching for her seat belt. "Yes, of course, I do."

* * *

He hadn't known the woman who now sat silently beside him at all. As silent as she, Edward faced that bitter fact as he drove back toward the center of town. Not necessarily because she had kept herself hidden from him, although the jury was still out on that one, but because he hadn't really looked.

He'd seen Jennie as warm and loving and happy, and he'd needed warmth and love and happiness in his life so much he hadn't bothered to look further. He hadn't bothered to learn why she cried for Rick who was left alone, not Ilsa who left, each time she watched that film. He hadn't bothered to learn why she allowed herself the release of tears only with the excuse of a sad movie.

He hadn't asked about her childhood, hadn't asked more than superficial questions about her college days or the beginning of her career. Maybe he was wise to ask if she had truly loved him, because, looking back, he suspected he hadn't done much to earn her love.

He, who had sworn never again to let himself be used, hadn't done much of anything, in fact, except use her. Take from her.

"Are we in the village again?"

Her softly spoken words startled him out of his reverie. "Yes. You knew?"

She gave him one of the smiles that had first drawn him to her, one of the smiles that he had only now begun to suspect often cost her dearly.

"The roadbed changed," she explained. "Are we back on a brick street?"

"You're very perceptive."

"So it seems."

He glanced at her in time to see her lips quirk in a grin. No. He saw no bitterness or pain in her eyes, only a wry humor. And how was he supposed to react to that? Make light of her condition? Or by not doing so, remind her of it?

"Yes," he said finally, choosing to do neither. "A brick street. We're about three streets over from the vicarage."

She found the power-window button and rolled down her window, then breathed deeply of the slightly cool, fragrantly scented air, before lapsing back into a silence until Edward broke it.

"I don't believe it," he said softly.

"What?"

"The iron fence we walked past yesterday? The one with the row of overgrown fir trees behind it blocking a view of the house?"

"Yes?"

"It's the next place on the list."

"Why do you sound so suspicious?" she asked, tuning right in to the cynicism he tried to keep from his voice.

"Coincidences, Jennie," he said. "You know I don't believe in them."

Coincidences, hell! he thought when he turned the Jeep into the driveway and passed the row of firs. *Jennie's house. The house she'd always dreamt of.*

I don't want a really big house, she'd told him once, a lifetime ago, grinning, teasing him. *Just a—a moderately big one. And old-fashioned. Maybe an Anne Hathaway-type English Tudor, with the half timbers but without the thatched roof. And a room on one end with windows all around where I can paint. And a big, homey kitchen and an upstairs and lots of room for kids.* Her voice had lost its teasing at that point. *Lots and lots of kids. You wouldn't mind that, would you, Edward? I really do want a house full of them. Ours. Really and truly ours.*

"What is it?" she asked. "What's wrong?"

"Wrong?" Edward shook his head to clear it and gave her a smile before he remembered she couldn't see it. "Did you ever think that you didn't just fall off a mountain,

Jennie, but that like Alice, you fell down the rabbit hole and brought all of us into Wonderland with you."

"Edward?"

The questions in her expressive eyes were too much for him to face at that moment; he had too many of his own. He released his seat belt but drew in a deep breath before reaching for the door latch. "It's all right, Jennie," he told her, knowing that it wasn't but not knowing how to make it so. "Let's go look at a house."

Eight

Jennie sat on an upholstered rattan chaise in a room warm with sunlight pouring in from three sides. She had slipped off her shoes and walked across the cool quarry-tile floor before sinking onto the seat against a wall of windows and tucking her feet beneath her. Edward stood beside her, turned toward the outside and, she supposed, he was looking through the windows. Now, truly comfortable, truly at home after touring a place she had never seen or been before, she felt free to question him.

"You're going to take it, aren't you?"

"I shouldn't. It's all wrong."

"Wrong for whom?" she asked. "Or should that be, wrong for what? Because it seems eminently right for you."

"It does, doesn't it?"

"And if you insist on moving part of your operations to town—I really wish you'd reconsider that, Edward." She knew why he was moving—only because she was here. "I really wish you wouldn't let me disrupt your life any more than I already have. But if you insist, this place is certainly large enough for you to have some sort of command post while Tim finds adequate offices for whatever crew you finally bring.''

"And I can get out of a hotel room and into a place of my own. I need that, Jennie."

"I understand," she told him, not knowing how but knowing she, too, had need for a place that was uniquely her own.

Edward hesitated, still facing the windows, then turned toward her. "I know you do. And you are the only one who ever has, the only one I've been able to admit that to—to admit any weakness to—in more years than I care to remember.''

Surprised by his words but sensing he had more locked within him that should be said, Jennie sat very still. Then, realizing that he, and probably she, had been locked in isolation much too long, she gathered her skirt from the seat beside her and held out her hand to Edward, inviting him to sit.

"Why?" she asked.

He took her hand and after a moment's hesitation, he sat beside her. "Why have I guarded myself? Why have I held myself aloof? Why have I been alone?''

And why did she feel an echo of all those actions deep within herself?

His hand tightened on hers. She heard a subtle change in his breathing, as though he was preparing for a painful confrontation. His voice held a slight catch as he started to speak, then stopped.

"It's no secret," he said at last. "Lambert knows. I'm sure the vicar knows by now. All my associates. Anyone who was in San Francisco when it happened. At one time, you knew.''

Knew what?

"I'm a very wealthy man," he told her. "It's not something I can take a lot of credit for—my family has always had a knack for knowing where, when and in what to invest and how to make our businesses thrive.

"I was born to it. I took it for granted until I was all of ten years old and someone, probably more than one someone, decided they were more entitled to what my family had accumulated than we were. I should have been with them, but I wasn't. I got left at home. As a punishment. God! I don't even know now what I did to make my father angry. He was never angry. Not with me or my sister, Megan, or with my mother, whom he loved so much that even I could see it."

His pain was palpable, so real Jennie felt the weight of it through their clasped hands. "Edward—you don't have to—"

"Yes. I do. Jennie, you didn't leave me. I know that now. But I have to tell you why I even considered believing that you did."

She nodded once, abruptly, silently urging him on.

"The ransom demand for my family was two million dollars, not an impossible amount considering our holdings, but difficult to come up with in the short amount of time the kidnappers gave us. The FBI said it probably wouldn't do any good to pay the money—I wasn't supposed to hear that, but I was damned sure not going to go off to my room and not know what was being done.

"It turned out they were right. We never saw my parents alive again, never found my sister's body."

"Oh, my God."

"I was placed under the guardianship of my father's sister and her husband. To say that I was a problem child is a vast understatement, but it wouldn't have mattered. 'Be a man,' my uncle kept telling me. 'Act like a man instead of a sniveling brat.' And I tried. God, how I tried. But the truth was, the only value I had to him was as the Carlton heir, and he did his best to see that there wasn't much left to inherit by the time I finally convinced a judge to look into his guardianship.

"The only value I had to a lot of people—women, relatives, employees, strangers on the street, was as the Carlton heir. Eventually, I got used to it. Eventually, I stopped looking for anything else and accepted that all of those people must be right."

"No, Edward. Oh, no."

He didn't hear her. His voice seemed to be coming from far away. As far away as his thoughts?

"That's why, at first, I didn't believe you could be real. And then, when I began to believe, when I began to need your warmth and your love, I always held on to just a little of that suspicion to protect me from loving you too much.

"There was no ransom note, Jennie. I told Lambert that. I held on to that, too, like a drowning man holds on to a life raft, because when I got back to the apartment and found you gone and the safe open, my first fear was that history was repeating itself. But there was a note from you. Telling me that you'd left me. Telling me that you'd never loved me. Telling me you realized you'd made a mistake."

No! She wanted to cry the word aloud. She couldn't possibly have done that. But she didn't know, did she?

He took her hand in both of his, lightly caressing the uneven ridge on her fourth finger. "Do you how this happened?"

She shook her head. No, she didn't know that, either. It was just one of the many mysteries of her life. Mysteries, as bad as they were, which paled when she thought of those Edward had been forced to live through.

"Someone claiming to be you sent your rings back to me. Without the diamonds. I suspect it was the same person who forced you to write that note, because I know—I knew then if I'd only let myself believe it—that you could never have left that way, could never have said those things, even if you had felt them."

He placed her hand on her thigh and released it, then stood, distancing himself from her by more than just a physical separation. "I had to believe you'd left me, Jennie. That was the only way I could survive. And I'm sorry. So sorry."

He turned from her, and his footsteps on the tile floor echoed the isolation that surrounded him. And her.

"Edward?" *Leaving?* He was leaving her? While on one level, she knew he would never abandon her in the strange house, on another, she felt only a wild panic. Not again. She couldn't go through it again. "Edward!"

His steps halted. Slowly, oh, so slowly, he returned to her side. His fingers brushed across her cheeks, leaving wet trails. But hadn't he just told her she never cried?

"Don't cry, Jennie," he whispered harshly. "Oh, God, I never wanted to make you cry."

"Please," she said, reaching for him, wrapping her arms around his waist and hiding her face against his chest. "Oh, please." But whether she meant *Please, don't leave me,* or *Please don't hurt anymore,* or *Please, don't have stopped loving me,* she didn't know. All she knew was that she had to have his touch, had to have him holding her, had to have the illusion, if only for this brief time, of truly belonging with someone.

"Jennie," he murmured, telling her with his words that he understood her panic even less than she did. "Oh, Jennie. I'll keep you safe, I promise. We'll stay here until whoever did this to you is caught. Lambert's working on it. He's in contact with the San Francisco police and a private investigator. We'll find out who did this. I won't let you be hurt again. And I'll make it up to you. If it's the last thing I ever do, I'll make it up to you for not believing in you. For not searching for you."

For not loving me?

He'd told her he had loved her once, just as clearly as he'd told her he'd fought loving her. But had he? Had anyone ever loved her? And if Edward loved her once, was it possible he still did?

Love didn't survive problems of the kind they'd had.

It hadn't; it wouldn't; it couldn't.

How did she know that, except by experience?

And then she realized what else he had said. She pulled away from him, looking up, searching but not seeing his expression. "Surely, I—you... Surely, no one thinks I'm in any danger?"

He sat beside her on the chaise, gathering her to him and resting his cheek against her head. She stiffened in the embrace before she admitted to herself that in his arms was where she wanted to be, needed to be.

"Madeline had a...background check run on you...before the wedding," he said hesitantly. "I didn't know about it at the time. I wasn't happy with her when I did learn about it. I haven't seen it," he added quickly as she tried to turn in his arms. "But I'm glad now we have it, or that we will as soon as Paul Slater, the investigator, can get a copy to us, because maybe something in it will give us a clue as to who would do this to you."

"Someone in my past?" she asked, hearing the doubt in her words but knowing she had no knowledge with which to explain that doubt. "Someone I knew, or trusted or— or..."

"Or loved?" he finished for her. "I hope not. God, I hope not, Jennie. But if not, who? We have so few clues and too many bizarre coincidences, and time—the time that has elapsed since this happened—doesn't help."

She heard the front door open and slam shut and the purposeful tap of a woman's high-heeled shoes on the hardwood floor of the entry hall before they were muffled by the thickly padded rug Edward had described to her as an Aubusson. She felt him tense and then relax as he must have realized who had entered the house.

"What now?" he said, but more to himself than to her. She tried to pull away but he held her still. "It's only Madeline.

"Problems?" he asked when the footsteps reached the tile floor of the room where they waited.

A woman's soft, cultured voice answered. "You might say that. Gibbons from the Houston office is on the cellular phone. He insists it's urgent and something only you can handle. Knowing him," she added dryly, "it probably is."

Edward chuckled, but Jennie heard the strain in his voice and wondered if this woman, Madeline, could tell how hard he strove for humor. "Cut him some slack, Maddie. He's brilliant at what he does, even if he did sleep through women's lib."

"Not I, fearless leader. It seems that you give him more than enough without my aiding and abetting."

Edward sighed and released Jennie. "Where's the phone?" he asked as he rose to his feet.

"In the car. The power adapter seems to be stuck. I didn't want to risk breaking anything."

Edward dropped his hand to Jennie's shoulder. "This could take a few minutes," he said, "but I'll hurry. Madeline? Will you keep Jennie company while I see what's wrong in Houston?"

The woman remained silent for moments after Edward left the room. Then, still not speaking, she crossed to where Jennie sat and stood nearby. Jennie felt her presence, strangely ominous, and wondered at her silence. "Madeline?" she asked. "Is something wrong?"

"I don't know, Jennie. Why don't you tell me?"

Her voice was still soft, still cultured, but now it held none of the affection with which she had spoken to Edward.

"We weren't friends, were we?" Jennie asked, sensing that she had just made a vast understatement.

"Hardly. I thought you were a money-grubbing little parasite then. I still do. Unfortunately, Edward seems to think you're necessary for his happiness. Don't hurt him again."

The words were delivered dispassionately, made all the more ominous by their complete lack of expression. Jennie shrank from the venom in them.

"Don't hurt him again," Madeline repeated, "or you'll answer to me. Now, since we've had a nice visit, and we understand each other as well as we ever did, I'll go see if Edward needs any help with Gibbons's problem."

Edward was alone when he rejoined her. Only minutes had passed, but they were minutes Jennie never wanted to relive. Had she ever before known such hate as Madeline had just shown her? Had Edward's assistant always made her feelings known to Jennie? To Edward? Was Madeline right? Was she a money-grubbing little parasite? Could she hurt Edward?

"I'm sorry for the interruption," Edward said.

Jennie shook her head, attempting to clear it of her dark thoughts. "Were you able to resolve the Houston problem?"

"Yes. Here."

She felt the nudge of something against her hand. "What?"

"Your shoes. Never mind," he said lightly. "Stay seated." He knelt at her feet and slipped her sandals in place. "You never did like shoes. I'm surprised this is the first time I've seen you without them."

She grimaced. "Yes, well, after I'd lost them a few times, I decided it was safer to keep them on."

"You need to keep me around, then, Jennie. I'll always find your shoes for you."

And anything else I lose? Like myself?

She put a hand on his shoulder, needing to touch him. "Edward? Are you sure? You don't have to stay with me, you know."

His shoulder tensed under her touch. "Do you want me to, Jennie?"

Want him to? Yes. More than life itself, she wanted this man beside her. With him she could face anything—Madeline's animosity, the doubts about her safety that Edward had raised—even a sightless world with no memories. *Even if he only stayed because he felt responsible for her?*

"Jennie?"

The surprising vulnerability in his voice reminded her of Madeline's warning. Hurt him? Not intentionally, not ever. "Yes," she said, her voice small and hesitant. "Yes," she repeated with more strength. "Oh, yes."

The night was still and quiet, with only a faint breeze ruffling the sheer curtains of her bedroom windows. Jennie sat alone in the darkness, haunted by the face of a man she could see only in her dreams. Edward? Surely it was Edward.

She closed her eyes and embraced the memory of the dream she had just awakened from. Embraced the memory of the man in that dream. His eyes were dark, intense, in a finely sculpted face that was drawn tight with need. His hand, strong, long-fingered, dark against the white of the dress she wore, trembled as it touched the first tiny, silk covered button. She had no words to go with this memory. No name. No sense of time or place. Only a longing, a deep emptiness that cried out for an end to the loneliness, that cried out for completion.

But there was none. The dream had stopped there. The memory stopped there. Leaving her aching. Leaving her alone on the window seat in the dark of the night, rocking back and forth, holding herself, because there was no one else to hold her. Because *he* wasn't there to hold her.

Edward forced himself to wait until just after breakfast the next morning before arriving on the minister's doorstep. Jennie, beautiful as ever in another of those gauzy dresses she now wore, looked as though she hadn't slept any better than he had. After exchanging only pleasantries with Reverend and Mrs. Winthrop, he took the picnic basket a smiling Matilda Higgins brought from the kitchen and led Jennie from the house, into the sunlight.

"A picnic?" she asked. "How did Caitlin know to pack a basket? You didn't say anything about a picnic yesterday."

He hadn't said much of anything; in fact, he'd just brought her into the house and stood looking down at her in silence, trying to find answers he knew weren't there. Then, knowing he was dangerously close to frightening her with the force of his need for her, he'd taken her face in his hands for long seconds before placing a too-brief kiss on her lips.

"It was an afterthought," he said, sounding well pleased with himself. "A pretty good one, I think."

"Yes," she agreed, lowering her window and breathing deeply of the early-morning air. "Where are we going?"

"Someplace ours, Jennie. A place where we won't be interrupted, no matter how well-meaning those interruptions are."

He hadn't realized how good it would feel to say those words until just that moment. There had been no privacy for them, not even alone in his car.

"Is that possible?" she asked with the lilt of a laugh in her voice.

"As of four o'clock yesterday afternoon, yes."

"You took the house?"

"I took it. It will be a few days before it's ready for me to move in, but for now, at least, I have the only keys to the gate, and I've told everyone we're going to be completely out of touch for the entire day."

Edward unpacked the picnic hamper and stowed the perishables in what he described to her as the largest non-commercial refrigerator he had ever seen. "It's vintage," he said, with dry humor lightening his words. "With cooling coils on top, metal racks and glass doors and door catches that haven't been put on home boxes in over twenty years."

But after saying that, he seemed lost. "Outside," he said abruptly, breaking the uneasy silence. "There's a fish pond, and a herb garden. Let's—yes. Let's go outside for a while."

He paused for a moment on their way outside. Only later, when they had reached the pond, did Jennie realize he had stopped to pick up a quilt, which he now spread on the grass. "Mrs. Higgins sent it with the basket. For the picnic," he explained.

Jennie nodded and sank to her knees on the quilt. After a moment, Edward joined her. *I'll always find your shoes for you.* Smiling at the memory of his words, she slipped off her sandals and curled her feet under her, arranging her voluminous skirt over her like a blanket.

The water from the fountain that fed the fish pond bubbled gaily and splashed over rocks on its way down to the small pond. Nearby, tender new leaves rustled in trees, and the branches swayed lightly, casting alternating patterns of sunlight and shadow over them. Birds foraging for their breakfast called to each other. And a delicate floral aroma perfumed the air.

The morning was just about perfect, except for the tension Jennie felt settle between the two of them.

Strangers wouldn't be so restrained. Strangers, at least, would be trying to communicate.

Strangers wouldn't have all the uncertainties of their troubled past, nor the doubts about their future, doubts that Edward had to feel every bit as strongly as she did. And, could their silence be attributed to the vulnerability he, too, must feel at exposing his emotions to someone who might not cherish them?

Suddenly, the quilt on which they sat was both too intimate and not—never—intimate enough a setting.

Quickly, carelessly, Jennie slipped into her shoes, rose and walked toward the sound of the fountain.

"Jennie?"

He stopped behind her. For the space of a heartbeat, he rested his hand on her shoulder then dropped it to his side.

She stood in shadow—always in shadow: her vision, her memories, her life. But one thing was very clear as she stood there. This was her dream all over. Not the setting. Not the time. But the emptiness. The terrible longing. And the man? Please, God, was he the same, too?

She turned toward him and found him even closer than she had thought. Resolute now, though trembling with a need she couldn't begin to explain, she lifted her face to his, trying to see, trying to sense, trying to *know*. When looking did no good, she raised her hands to his face, tracing the lines of cheek and forehead and lips. Were they the same? They were, weren't they?

And now she felt him tremble.

"Edward?"

"Yes, Jennie," he said with a harsh kind of gentleness.

They were both vulnerable, both hurting. Someone had to make the first effort. Someone had to be willing to risk—to risk . . .

"Edward, I want you to kiss me."

Now he lifted his hands to her face, holding her still.

"The way you would have kissed me in the Winthrops' garden," she said when he remained silent. "If Jamie hadn't interrupted. The way your touch and your silence and the tension between us tell me you want to, now."

His words were almost a groan. "Jennie, I can't."

Wrong. She had been wrong. But she had been so sure. *As sure as she had been before, so many times before?*

She felt all her strength leave her. Still, she managed to keep her chin up, her shoulders straight as she withdrew her hands from Edward's face. "I'm sorry," she said. "Obviously I was mistaken."

He wouldn't let her go. She felt his hands clench on her shoulders as she tried to step away from him.

"If I kiss you, I won't want to stop. And we're not ready for that, are we?"

Were they? "And if we aren't now, will we ever be? With me locked in a world I can't remember, unable even to explore memories with you? You said I loved you. You said you loved me. But did we ever make love, Edward? I don't even have that to hold on to." But did she? Wasn't that what her dream was? A memory her conscious mind would not, could not, allow her to have?

"Once," he said, shaking her briefly, sounding almost angry. "Only once. On our wedding day. It was the first time for you. As jaded as I was, it felt like the first time for me, too."

She sagged against him in relief. Her first time. With him. Oh, yes, it was Edward in her dreams. Thank God, it was Edward in her dreams.

She felt a tear slip from her eye. Damn! For someone once able to cry only at sad movies, she was setting new records. He traced his finger across her cheek, stealing the tear, and she knew that she had to expose even more of herself to him if they were to have a future.

Once again she lifted her hands to his face. "You have dark hair," she said softly. "Almost black. And equally dark eyes but with flecks of gold and green in them. And high cheekbones with dark, almost permanently tanned-looking, skin. And a small, old scar, really no more than a tiny, white line, here—'' She traced a space at his temple, just at the hairline. ''And I wanted you more than anything or anyone I had ever wanted, more than my next breath, more than my life if you weren't in it.''

He sucked in a harsh breath, and for a moment she was afraid she had just made the largest mistake of her life. Then he wrapped her in his arms with a strength that forced the air from her.

''God, Jennie, when I came back to the apartment and found you gone, I felt as though my heart had been ripped out of me. It had been. Because without you, I hadn't had one. Only the shell of a body that went through the motions of life without feeling. Without allowing myself to feel.

''And the pain of losing you after a lifetime of emptiness was more than I could bear. I had to shut it off.''

''Edward. Oh, Edward.'' She stopped his torrent of words with her fingers on his lips. ''I understand,'' she told him with a watery chuckle. ''I of all persons have to understand.''

''Yes. Yes.'' She felt his breath against her cheek as he lifted her to him. ''But you always understood. How could I have let myself forget that?''

''Hush,'' she whispered. ''Just hold me.'' *Hold me. Kiss me. Make love to me. Never let me go. Never leave me.* Leave her? How could she think this man would ever leave her? He needed her as much as she needed him. Of that much she was sure. Just as she was sure he was still fighting expressing that need.

''Oh, Edward,'' she whispered, knowing that in this, too, she must go first. ''Edward.''

With a gentle sigh, she found his mouth, first with her fingers, then with soft, exploring lips.

He tensed at her touch and then, as though sensing the inevitability of what must follow, he surrendered to the need she had felt in him. "Yes," he moaned as he opened his mouth to her gentle onslaught, as he stopped fighting his need and began sharing it with her. "Oh, yes."

Nine

———

Edward carried her into the house and up the stairs to a room that was dim and cool. Slowly, as though she were the most precious thing in the world to him, he lowered her to a wide bed covered with what felt like a hand-crocheted coverlet.

As he pulled away from her, she reached up, catching his arms, and pulling him back to her. She felt the bed dip slightly with his added weight, and then he was beside her, his lips moving over her cheek, her throat.

"Jennie. Oh, Jennie," he murmured. "I thought we'd never be together again."

"I know," she said, "I know." Her breath caught as his hand skimmed to cup her breast. How could someone as strong as Edward, as powerful as he, be so gentle? How had he, in a world without love, learned to show her how much he cherished her touch? And how had she survived without him?

She hadn't. She had merely existed. In a world without color. But now Edward—with his touch, with his whispered words of endearment, with the increasingly demanding movement of his body against hers, with the caress of his lips bringing her to an almost feverish awareness of how much had been stolen from them—Edward was giving her color, was giving her life.

He hesitated only once, paused above her at the moment of joining, ready to make her his and yet, at that moment, seeming reluctant to do so. She reached for his face, tracing her fingers along its sharp planes, seeing it as she had in her dream, drawn tight with need.

"I love you, Edward," she told him. "I always have. I always will. If I never know anything else about my life before Avalon, I know that." She lifted herself to him in silent supplication. With a moan torn from him, he made them one. And then, in an act of giving that brought more of those damnable tears to her eyes, he brought her to shattering fulfillment before finding his own release in what she could only think of as a worship of her body.

A soft breeze played through the room when Jennie awoke. She shifted slightly, listening to the faint birdsongs, and felt a solid steady warmth beside her.

Edward.

The memory of their morning of loving flooded her with warmth, with a welcome sense of its rightness. With knowing that here, with him, she belonged.

She turned toward his warmth and found him propped on one elbow beside her.

"I slept," she said softly, apologizing for leaving him even for that.

"I know. But I suspect you needed it after not sleeping last night."

She flushed slightly at the memory of how restlessly she'd slept last night, her dreams filled with Edward. "And just how did you know that?" she asked, grinning. The reality of Edward's touch had been much better than the dream.

"Because I didn't sleep, either," he told her. He traced a finger along her jawline, then lifted one of her short, tousled curls. "Or eat much breakfast."

As if answering a cue, Jennie's stomach gave a protesting growl. Edward laughed and planted a kiss on her forehead. "Wait here. We do have food."

"Wait!"

Edward paused in pushing himself up from the bed.

"Is that the best you can do in the way of a good-morning kiss?" she asked with a mock pout.

"Imp." He laughed, and the sound was young, gay and full of male satisfaction. "That's the only kiss I dare give you if I expect to get any food before this day is over."

While Edward was gone on his food run, Jennie ran her hands over the crocheted coverlet. Was it as gorgeous as it felt? Shaking her head, she got out of bed, intent on straightening the spread. After a few frustrating moments, she stopped, laughing at herself. She supposed she could make the bed by touch, but with the linens as disturbed as they had become with their lovemaking, and now, with her efforts to straighten them, she wasn't sure how it would look. She settled for tugging the bottom sheet into place and popping the top one out, letting it float into place. She then piled the pillows at the head of the bed and herself against the pillows, relishing the feel of fine, soft cotton on her bare skin. Her bare, well-loved skin.

Should she be embarrassed? Was her body something she had always kept covered? Was it—was it blemished? Marked in any way from all that had happened to her? Would Edward think she was flaunting herself—

Stop it!

If Edward had found her body in any way displeasing, he'd certainly hidden that from her.

And if she'd ever thought she should hide it, the pleasure Edward took in it should have driven that notion completely out of her mind.

Still—

"Some *femme fatale* I am," she muttered as she tugged the top sheet up to cover herself.

"Yeah. That you are."

She hadn't heard him return. Now his soft laugh had the heat rising to stain her cheeks. "You weren't supposed to hear that," she said, tucking the sheet firmly around her.

"And you're not supposed to be embarrassed."

She jerked her head around to face the doorway. "Yes—well," she said, feeling her chin going up defiantly. Giving a rueful laugh, she relaxed against the pillow and found a smile for him. "Perhaps you can tell me just what I am supposed to do?"

"That's easy," he said as he placed a tray on the bed beside her. "You're supposed to tell me what a fantastic lover I am and how I make you *feel* like a *femme fatale*."

"Oh. Is that what I did before?"

"No." His voice hovered in the air above her, full of the strain she had been foolish enough to hope was gone forever. "No," he repeated. "It's what you tried to do, and I wouldn't let you."

Suddenly chilled, Jennie tried to tug the sheet higher.

"Here," Edward said after a moment. "Lean forward."

As she did so, not questioning, she felt the whisper of soft cotton across her shoulders and smelled the unique aroma of fine soap and after-shave and Edward. "Your shirt?"

"Yes." He tugged the collar up to frame her throat and captured her face with his hands. Had he banished his demons so easily? Jennie wondered. He must have, because the easy teasing she could grow to like too much was back in his voice and in his words.

"It looks a lot better on you than it does on me," he said. He lifted the tray and placed it across her lap, carefully balancing the tray's legs on each side of her, before sliding into bed beside her. "Of course, *nothing* looked a lot better on you than that shirt does on me, too."

She must not be accustomed to compliments, she thought, or flirtation, because she felt the heat rise again to her face. Edward chuckled and dropped his arm over her shoulder, hugging her quickly. "I don't know about you," he said, "but I'm going to have to eat if I want to keep up my strength."

Eat. Yes, well, now this was going to be interesting. Jennie hesitated, knowing too well the potential for disaster in what should be such a simple task.

"Jennie?"

She felt his hand touch hers—a light, encouraging brush of his fingers only across the back of the fist she had unknowingly closed.

This is Edward, she told herself. Edward, with whom she had just let herself be her most vulnerable. Edward, with whom she would trust her life. What was a little embarrassment compared to what they had already shared? She looked at him and shrugged. "I'm sorry," she said. "What wonderful things do we have for lunch?"

Later, she realized she was going to have to hug Caitlin, or Matilda, or both of them. Lunch was wonderful: filling enough for Edward, and yet prepared in such a way that Jennie had no problems, no embarrassing spills, no uncomfortable moments. Of course, Edward's gentle teasing attitude had something to do with that. Had she seen behind the stern, unsmiling man to this side of him before? Had anyone other than she *ever* seen this side of him?

After lunch, replete and relaxed, Edward set the tray aside and they lay back against the pillows with stemmed glasses of a fine, light wine. He had once again draped his arm over her shoulder, and now he held her close to his side, periodically leaning even closer to nuzzle his face against her hair or just to clasp her in a brief, tight embrace.

And they talked. Had they talked like this before?

Had *Edward* ever talked like this before? With her? With anyone? Sharing his plans for the *Lady B* now that he had regained her. Sharing his hopes for a life filled with more than the running of Carlton Enterprises. Sharing his pain and his grief as a ten-year-old who had lost his entire world.

And she? She talked of the color and shape that filled her dreams. Talked of the man—Edward, she now knew—who had filled them from the time she awoke in the hospital, alone and frightened and not knowing who she was. Talked of how the love of the townspeople had first frightened her because it seemed so alien to what she should expect.

Talked of an emptiness within her that she had never been able to understand until Edward had filled that emptiness.

Talked of teasing the man in her dreams, even knowing she flirted with danger to do so, so that she could coax from him a smile that even in her dreams she knew was rare.

"Did I tease you, Edward?" she asked.

He coughed, which Jennie recognized as an attempt to choke back a laugh. "Constantly," he told her. "Your purpose in life for the first few weeks after I met you seemed to be to shake me up and out of my image of myself as the mature, all-knowing, correct person in our relationship."

"Oh." After one of her dreams, she had compared what she did to baiting a tiger. Yes, she had definitely been doing something very similar. "Did I succeed?" she asked.

He rested his cheek against her hair and spoke softly, reflectively. "The name Renn. What does it mean to you?"

Nothing. No more than the name Edward. But she had spoken it twice and knew it had to be important. She moved her head gently against his cheek in a negative gesture.

"You hated my name," he told her. "Or maybe what it stood for. 'Edward William Renberg Carlton IV,' you once said, 'is a fitting name for an entire law firm, not for just one man.' And I do believe you hated the persona I sometimes wore with that name. 'Pompous,' you called it. Of course, you were right.

"One day when I was in my mature and correct mode and attempting to drag you in there with me, you pointed to a flock of birds feeding in the park near your apartment. Wrens. Hundreds of them.

"'Strutting little brown birds,' you said. 'So full of themselves. So like you in moments like this.' Then you laughed and extracted that portion of my name. 'Of course,' you told me. 'Someone else must have seen the similarity, generations back.'

"From then on, whenever I became too staid, too stodgy, too full of myself, you dragged that name out, reminding me but with no one else ever knowing of what, exactly what you thought of my attitude."

"And you continued to see me?" she asked.

"Oh, Jennie," he told her. "By then I *had* to continue to see you."

"Had to?" Why was it so difficult to believe that someone had needed her so much?

"Had to," he repeated, turning her in his arms. "Had to eat. Had to breathe. Had to have Jennie in my life." His voice caught as she turned and pressed her face against his chest. With a hand that trembled slightly, a long-fingered, slender, and, she knew, tanned hand, he lifted her chin, raising her face to his. "Just as right now, I have to make love to you again."

Jennie was silent on the drive back to the minister's house that afternoon. A day of love does not a reconciliation make, she thought, but she did take some consolation that Edward was not particularly overjoyed by the prospect of returning her to the vicarage, either. And then she wondered why the word *reconciliation* had come so easily to her mind. Reconciliation implied, at least on one level, forgiveness. Neither of them had done anything to require forgiveness.

And it also implied compromise. Oh, yes. And she suspected that if she and Edward were to resume their life together there would have to be a lot of that. Already, he was embroiled in so many changes because of her. There would be more, she knew. There would have to be, because of her condition, because of the questions surrounding what had happened, and because—well, just because Edward was who he was. Stalwart. Yes. That was definitely a good description of him. She suspected he had always been. And she—

Jennie felt a quick chill shudder through her. She was not the same as she had been. Might never be again. In spite of Dr. Freede's assurances that her memory could return at any moment. But what about her sight? No one seemed to know. No one even seemed to want to speculate, past the point of suggesting that the neurosurgeon who was scheduled to arrive soon as a consultant might have answers the entire medical staff of Avalon Hospital had not been able to find.

And if she did somehow miraculously regain her memory *and* her sight, would she ever again be the innocent girl with whom Edward had fallen in love?

Would she ever again feel free enough or young enough to tease him into life when that was called for? Would she ever again be as sure of who and what and why she was as the woman he had described with such loving memory?

"Damn," Edward muttered as he slowed and braked to a stop.

"What is it?" At last something had brought her out of her reverie, but would anything that brought that dark tone to Edward's voice be any more pleasant?

"We're at the vicar's house," he told her. "And so is your friend, the sheriff."

"Sheriff Lambert?" She shook her head. Surely that wasn't male jealousy she heard. "He has been a good friend to me, Edward. But no more than anyone else in Avalon."

"Right."

She heard the click as he released his seat belt.

"Edward." She laid her hand on his arm, stopping him as he opened his door. "What's wrong."

He hesitated, then covered her hand with his, clasping it lightly. "He's either here to make sure I haven't hurt you in some way," he told her, "or he has news. Either way, the next few minutes have the possibility of being uncomfortable for you."

"And you?"

"Of course not," he said lightly, patting her hand before he released it and stepped from the car. "I'll just go into my CEO mode. Nothing can get through that."

Maybe he'd meant his words only to tease, but they did not reassure her because they cut too close to what she suspected he had done all his life. Jennie hesitated as she clasped the seat-belt release. And what about herself? Did she have a protective mode to go into if the sheriff's news became too uncomfortable? Would she need one?

Edward opened her door and she realized that no matter how much she suddenly feared facing what awaited them in the vicar's pleasant home, face it she must.

Mrs. Winthrop met them in the entry hall and directed them to the front parlor before excusing herself. As Edward had suspected, Lambert rose from one of the wingback chairs when they entered, and he did not look happy. He studied Jennie silently for a moment, and Edward knew he couldn't fail to see that she had changed. Her eyes glowed, and her body seemed to radiate a new assurance.

In other words, she looked like a woman who was loved. Who knew she was loved. Who had recently *been* loved.

"Miss Jennie," he said. "Carlton."

"Sheriff Lambert." Jennie gave the man a dazzling smile. "How nice of you to come by. Is Jamie with you?"

A small tick near the sheriff's temple and his curt nod toward Edward were the only signs he made as he acknowledged Edward's claim.

"No," he said. "She asked me to tell you she'd be by later." His voice softened when he spoke to Jennie. Hell, Edward thought, Lambert's voice always softened when he spoke to Jennie. "I'm sorry, but this is an official call. Would you mind very much excusing us so that I can talk with—" he glanced at Edward "—your husband?"

Edward felt Jennie's fingers tighten on his arm at the same moment he saw her chin go up.

"If you mean," she said with a quiet strength, "would I mind leaving so that the two of you can discuss my past and my future, then my answer must be, of course, I would. Don't you think it's time to start including me in these conversations?"

Again Lambert glanced at Edward. He didn't want her here, didn't want her upset any more than Edward did, but like Edward, he seemed to realize that Jennie needed to be included. Edward guided her to one of the wing chairs but when she had seated herself, she refused to release his hand, refused to let him leave her side.

When he had seated himself on the arm of the chair and Lambert had resumed his position in the opposite one, Edward noticed the opened express-delivery envelope that rested on the table by the sheriff.

"Slater's report?" Edward asked and felt Jennie's fingers tighten on his.

Lambert nodded. "Miss Jennie," he said, "before your marriage, Ms. Harrison—she's Mr. Carlton's assistant—had a private investigator look into your background."

"I know," Jennie said. "Edward told me. Yesterday. But he couldn't tell me what the report said. Is it— Have you—"

"Yes, it's here. And yes, I've read it."

He glanced at Edward. Did the man really think Edward would object or challenge him for the right to be the one to give this report to Jennie?

When Edward only nodded, Lambert picked up the envelope. "There is absolutely nothing in your past to be ashamed of, Miss Jennie," he said, homing in on what Edward had suspected was one of Jennie's greatest, though unspoken fears. "No deep dark secrets, no arrest record, not even any suspect behavior. Paul Slater told us you were squeaky-clean. This report corroborates that."

Her fingers still dug into his; her body still radiated tension. "So there is nothing—nothing to indicate that something I did—someone I knew—did this...."

Lambert shook his head. "No."

"Tell me," Jennie said. She drew a deep breath and leaned forward. "Tell me about me. Please."

"Are you sure?" Edward asked. "Shouldn't we ask Dr. Freede before we go poking around in your past?"

"I asked," Lambert said. "He said it was all right as long as Jennie didn't get too upset."

"Besides," Jennie said, gently chiding, "you two have already been poking around in my past. I'm the only one who doesn't know what's going on. Tell me," she said.

Lambert didn't bother to take the papers from the envelope. "*You're* squeaky clean," he said. "I want you to remember that. Because there are some things, early on, things completely out of your control, that might cause you a little—a little discomfort, just hearing them cold like this."

She looked as though she were bracing to be struck. Edward draped his arm over her shoulder and rubbed her arm, softly, comforting her in the only way he felt she would accept.

"Tell me," she repeated.

Lambert nodded. "You were the only child of a single mother who never revealed who your father was."

Edward felt Jennie flinch, but she remained silent.

"Apparently, your mother loved you very much," Lambert said. "She kept you, cared for you. She did have to put you in day care while she worked. When you were not quite three, she was killed by a mugger when she was leaving her office after working late.

"Because you had no other family, you were placed under the care of the state. When you were five, you were adopted, but just before the adoption was finalized, your adoptive family went on a camping trip. You were involved in a massive freeway pileup. The man who was to become your father was killed, your mother seriously injured, both physically, and, according to Slater's report, emotionally. Her mother persuaded her to cancel the adoption. You were sent back, and lived in a series of foster homes, apparently with unremarkable results—certainly no problems—until you graduated from high school and won an art scholarship to college.

"There, there was one questionable episode. In your junior year, you accused your major adviser of sexual harassment. In the ensuing publicity and controversy, he was exonerated of your charges. A year after that, three other young women came forward to accuse that professor of similar advances and pressures, one of them going so far as to file criminal charges, of which he was convicted.

"But you had already changed schools for your senior year, losing your scholarship. You supported yourself during that last year as a cook in a pizza place popular with the students and shared a nearby apartment with two other art students, a young man working on his master's degree, and a young woman you described as very talented but who was just starting her classes.

"After graduation, you began teaching elementary school and painting, and soon you and your two room-mates moved into a larger apartment and the three of you lived there for about two years, until you moved into the studio you occupied when you met Mr. Carlton."

"Why?" she asked. "Why did I move? Was there a fight, or..."

And why was Jennie suddenly so damned insecure? Edward glared at Lambert, defying him to cause her any more pain, but Lambert only smiled. "On the contrary," the sheriff said. "There was a wedding. Between your room-mates. A part of your gift to them was your lease, and their privacy.

"Without exception, your neighbors, former co-workers and associates describe you as a warm and generous friend, without an enemy. There's no trace of envy, anger or dissension in any of your relationships, except with your student adviser."

"And he—" Edward leaned forward. "Where has he been these past few months."

Lambert shook his head. "He had a stroke during his trial. He's never completely recovered. He's living with a grown daughter now, on the East Coast, and while anything is possible, he's pretty much out of the picture as a viable suspect."

"So everybody loves me," Jennie said in a small voice that immediately drew Edward's attention to her, to the resolute set of her shoulders, to the defiant tilt of her chin, to the sheen of moisture in her eyes. "If so," she asked, "why didn't anyone search for me? If I was such a good friend, why didn't anyone ask why I didn't call or visit? Did they get notes, too?"

"No," Lambert said. "Jennie—damn!—Edward, do you know if Jennie had made any plans to close her apartment or move her studio?"

"No, she hadn't. We'd talked about it, and she'd decided to keep the studio as a place to work."

"I thought as much, based on what you'd said earlier."

"Jennie, your neighbors all knew about your wedding and were happy for you. That's why they weren't surprised to see a moving van at your studio the day of the wedding—"

Edward felt her small start—of surprise? or dismay?—before Lambert continued. "Edward told me he went to your studio after you disappeared and found it empty.

"Your landlady was told that you were moving everything to the Carlton estate outside of town until you decided where you would live and work."

"And my paintings? My—my things?"

"In order to speed things up, I've had Paul Slater looking into what happened. Thanks to a neighbor of yours, he was able to locate the moving company. The order to move was given by someone using the name J. A. Long. Everything was moved to a warehouse storage facility, one of those lock-and-keep-the-key places, in San Diego, where the rent had been paid for three months.

"There are no paintings left, but Slater found the place in time to stop a scheduled sale of the rest of your possessions."

Edward felt the defeat struggling to overcome her, but Jennie held herself erect. Even if she couldn't remember it now, her work had been her life before he entered it. "And my paintings?"

Lambert looked at the framed watercolor over the mantel and then to Edward. For permission? Edward doubted it. Lambert didn't appear to be the type to ask permission for much of anything. But for assurance that Edward would help brace Jennie against whatever his next words evoked? Possibly. Slowly, knowing what had to follow, Edward nodded.

"A man purporting to be a collector of your work has been selling them one or two at a time across the country. We don't have a positive ID on him yet, but he appears to fit the description of the former security guard at Edward's San Francisco apartment."

"But how—who—"

"Reverend Winthrop's daughter bought one from him in San Diego, Miss Jennie, as a Christmas present for the reverend. She said that the man who sold it began a conversation with her in a gallery she frequented. He eventually told her he had to raise some quick cash because of a tax problem. She also said that he seemed fascinated when she told him she had grown up in New Mexico. Of course, believing Avalon to be a fascinating place, she hadn't thought too much about that part of the conversation until I began asking questions about her purchase."

"A painting?" she said. "One of my paintings? Here? Where?"

"Over the mantel," Edward said.

"In this room?" Suddenly, Jennie sprang to her feet. "All this time there has been one of my paintings in this room. And—and you knew and didn't say anything."

"Jennie." Edward rose to his feet and dropped his hands onto her shoulders, stilling her. "No one knew until I arrived. And no one knew what to say after I arrived. It seemed a cruelty, a mockery that—"

She shrugged away from his touch and made her way to the fireplace. Slowly, tentatively, she raised her hand to the frame, to the glass that protected the work. "A watercolor?" she asked. "Is it one I sold or— Of course. No one knows. No one but I could know. She traced her fingers along the glass until she reached the frame. "What is it? What's the subject?"

"The *Lady B,*" Edward told her.

Jennie's hand fisted over the glass. Head bowed, she stood there silently for one second, two, a third, before straightening to her full height and whirling to confront the two men.

"I would not have sold this painting."

Ten

I would not have sold this painting.

Jennie's words lingered in Edward's memory as he closed the door to the vicarage and started down the sidewalk in the shadowy twilight of early evening. She'd repeated them to him as he stood with her at the base of the stairs only moments before. "I wouldn't have, Edward. I don't know how or why I know, but I wouldn't have."

He hadn't argued to take her with him when he left; she hadn't argued to go. But the embrace they shared was intense, almost desperate, before she tore herself away from him and hurried up the stairs.

He heard a noise ahead and tensed but found only Lambert leaning back against the fender of his Land Rover with one elegantly booted foot propped on the sidewall of the tire.

"I suspected you weren't through with me," Edward said.

Lambert nodded but remained in his curiously alert slouch against the vehicle. "Is she all right?"

"Sure," Edward said. "She's top of the form. Fine and dandy. *How the hell do you think she is?*"

"Resilient," Lambert said in his slow drawl. "A lot sturdier than any of us want to give her credit for being. And brave. My God, that is one brave woman. How are you?"

"She is, isn't she?" Slowly, Edward released his anger. Lambert didn't deserve it; he was only doing his job. And if the sheriff noticed that Edward hadn't answered his question, he kept silent. "You have no idea who did this to her, do you?"

Lambert straightened away from his car. "Let's walk a while," he said.

Edward hesitated, then nodded and fell into step with the sheriff as they walked the brick sidewalks of Avalon.

"When are you moving into the house?" Lambert asked after a few minutes of silent walking.

"Soon," Edward told him, wondering at the change of topic but also welcoming it, for the moment.

"You were there today."

"Yes." He might as well admit it. The man obviously knew the answer. "I wanted a place where Jennie and I wouldn't be interrupted. We needed—we needed some privacy."

"Yes. You did." Again Lambert lapsed into what might have been mistaken for a companionable silence. "Tomorrow would be a good day for a move," he said at last. "I understand the place is habitable."

"Yes." Edward glanced at Lambert to gauge his mood. *Habitable?* If the estate was on either of the coasts, the owners could sell tours. Except for a few mundane things, unfortunately some of which were needed for daily living, the house and grounds were complete, and just about perfect.

"Marianna Richards can help bring it up to your standards," Lambert told him. "She was a high-powered interior designer before she married and returned to Avalon. She also can help you find a competent staff for the house. No matter how long you stay, a house this size will require a staff."

"Thanks. I'll remember that."

They had almost reached the gates of the house in question when Lambert stopped. "Must be getting close to dinnertime," he said, turning and heading back toward the vicar's house at a no more determined pace than the one that had carried them there.

"What does your crew think of the food at the lodge?"

Edward raised an eyebrow in question. Lambert did this slow-talking southern, good-old-boy routine extremely well. Unfortunately, he'd already shown Edward a different facet of his personality. "Since they're all reasonably competent," he said, affecting a drawl of his own, "they understand that it's exceptionally good."

Lambert turned his head and grinned. "Good. Then they won't think anything's out of line if you invite me to dinner with you, will they?"

Edward stopped, looking at the sheriff, wondering when he had lost the thread of the conversation.

"So I can be there when you tell them. About the move."

Damn! "You're still suspicious of my people?" he asked. "I've told you, I trust them implicitly. And all the background checks we've run on them show them to be almost as clean as—"

"As Jennie?" Lambert smiled grimly. "Perhaps it is someone in her past," he conceded, "someone Slater didn't pick up on. But for now, humor me. I'm not going to accuse anyone of anything tonight, just observe. And have some—how did you describe it?—exceptionally good food."

* * *

Madeline was still upstairs, dressing for dinner, but the men were already gathered in the lounge when Edward and Lambert arrived in their separate vehicles. Edward left the sheriff with his staff and excused himself to shower and change.

He'd just left his room to return to the lounge when Madeline caught up with him.

"What is it, Madeline? Don't tell me Gibbons has gone berserk again."

She shook her head and studied him carefully. "Are you all right? I was—am—concerned about you. I know these past few days have been hard on you, Edward. And today... What can I say to convince you that you don't have to do this to yourself? She isn't worth it."

"Maddie—" His first impulse was to tell her that whatever he did, Jennie was well worth it. That whatever he did, the decision was his and not Madeline's. But that wouldn't have been fair to say to her. Madeline had been his assistant since he assumed control after finishing college. She was family, although distant, and friend, and the total of all those was more, much more than the three of them separately. "Thanks," he said. "Thanks for worrying. And thanks for understanding."

Lucas Lambert had taken a relaxed position near the huge stone fireplace, and the men were seated in the oversize leather chairs near him, each nursing a before-dinner drink. Conversation was light. Tim Huxton was in the middle of a trout-fishing story Edward had heard in many incarnations but always enjoyed because Tim was never too proud to put himself as the object of ridicule, and this story reached new heights of the ridiculous each time it was told.

The story spun to its conclusion and Lambert looked up in laughter to see Edward and Madeline enter the room.

He saw Lambert's eyes light in male appreciation of Madeline Harrison's sleek and sophisticated beauty. Well,

Edward thought, well, well. Imagine that. The man was just as susceptible to her as every other male in this town.

Dinner passed in easy conversation, far removed from Jennie and the mystery that had brought her here, and with only a few halfhearted groans when Edward, following Lambert's earlier suggestion, announced they would move their operations into the temporary headquarters at the house the following day.

After dinner, the men excused themselves one by one either to attend to work or to prepare for the next day, until only Edward, Madeline and Lambert remained in the lounge. Remembering one further item that must be handled, Edward followed Tim out to have a few more words with him.

Madeline was laughing gently at something Lambert said, when Edward returned, and Edward stopped, listening quietly. Paris. The sheriff was telling Madeline something about a trip to Paris and Madeline was leaning forward to listen closely. Unless Edward was mistaken, he saw more than an inveterate traveler's curiosity animating her cool beauty.

Edward leaned against the door facing, at last acknowledging the exhaustion and tension that once again gripped him. He was definitely not needed here. This was a male-female thing, not an interrogation, and he—whether it made sense to anyone else in the world or not—he owed Lucas something after today.

And maybe he owed Madeline something, too. Lambert was a good man. She could do worse.

Silently, Edward left the lounge without their ever knowing he had returned.

In his room, he opened the window and stood listening to the night sounds. Too many trees and too many hills separated him from Jennie for him to see even the town from where he stood, let alone to see the light from her window in that town, but for a moment he felt closer to her.

For a moment, he imagined her standing beside the windows in her room in a nightgown as soft and feminine as the dresses she wore gently draping her sweet curves, concealing yet revealing them in the moonlight.

Suddenly angry, frustrated, lonely and aching with wanting her, he swore violently. He'd been a fool to leave her there. He should have insisted she come back to the lodge with him.

And do what?

Stay locked up with him in his room while he lost himself in her?

Put herself on display at a public meal before people she couldn't remember?

Put herself in danger by leaving the walled protection of the vicar's house?

So everybody loves me, she'd said in a small voice that told him that she wanted to believe it, but she didn't, not for a moment. Because somebody obviously did not love Jennie.

I love you. She'd said that, too, with more force, with more conviction. Maybe she believed it. God knew, he wanted to. But now, away from her, away from the spell she always wove around him, old doubts rose to taunt him.

What would Jennie, full of light and life, want with him?

"Are you all right?" he asked her. *"Really all right? I didn't hurt you?"*

She grinned at him then. "One of my deepest, darkest secrets is this hidden desire I've had to be ravished by a loving madman. Edward?" She sat up in the bed, letting the sheet fall away from her as she captured his face in her small hands.

"Edward, I'm teasing you. Of course you didn't hurt me. You'd never do that."

But he would. She'd tire of his moods, tire of teasing him out of them, tire of his not being able to give anything of himself to her. He'd drain her of her light, of her life, and eventually, after he had grown completely dependent upon her, she'd have nothing left of herself, and nothing of him.

The dream came again that night, again awakening Jennie, again leaving her alone and aching as she sat on the window seat in the darkness of night.

This time there had been more. Prompted by the incredible day of loving she had spent with Edward? Or created from that day? She didn't know. How could she know?

She closed her eyes and surrendered to the enveloping darkness and slowly, so slowly, light filtered through the darkness, illuminating a stage on which there were only two players. Edward. Oh, yes, it was Edward. And someone she could not see, only feel the responses of.

Again his eyes were dark, intense, in a finely sculpted face that was drawn tight with need. His hand, strong, long-fingered, dark against the white of the dress she wore, trembled as it touched the first tiny, silk-covered button.

I love you, Jennie. His words were harsh with the same need she saw in his face. With the same need that had her shaking with longings she had never before experienced, with longings she knew must echo his. *I had to have you. Without you, there is no life, Jennie. Without you, there is only an emptiness so great I'll never find my way out.*

For her, too! Didn't he know that? Couldn't he see?

Couldn't she tell him?

Apparently not.

In her memory, in her dream, in her heart, she touched him. She drew his hand from the row of buttons to the soft swell of her breast and heard him suck in a deep breath. Then she felt his mouth on hers, claiming her with an intensity that could have—*would* have—frightened her, had she not felt it, too.

The time for words was past. They had wanted each other too much, waited too long, to be satisfied by words, to be appeased by anything less than all of each other.

She watched in amazement as hands that had to be hers tore at Edward's buttons, skimmed over tautly muscled shoulders, chest, abdomen, worked with increasing impatience at a stubborn belt.

She listened in amazement as a voice that had to be hers urged him on with wordless whispers and moans as his hands exposed more of her heated, needy body to his hands, to his mouth, to the increasingly urgent surges of his body against hers.

She felt in amazement the need that rocked her, even now, as those moments played out, as at the last moment, the moment of joining, how he tried to rein in the passion that drove him. *No!* she had cried silently then, cried silently now. *Don't hold yourself away from me! Don't keep anything of yourself from me! Can't you see I need you? Can't you see I need this!*

She had driven him on, feeling his shock when he discovered that he was her first lover, feeling his attempt, even then, once again to protect her, to shield her from his need. She hadn't let him. Not knowing where her knowledge had come from, she had touched and tempted and taunted until he was again as lost in need as she, until she felt the magic, the wonder of completion, hers and his, and he sank beside her, holding her, oh, yes, holding her gently, lovingly, forever in his arms.

And then—something—*what?*—had happened to shatter their closeness.

"Are you all right?" he'd asked her. She remembered that, but not how he had come to be standing over her, dressed. *"Really all right? I didn't hurt you?"*

She grinned at him then. *"One of my deepest, darkest secrets is this hidden desire I've had to be ravished by a loving madman. Edward?"* She sat up in the bed, letting the sheet fall away from her as she captured his face in her hands.

"Edward, I'm teasing you. Of course you didn't hurt me. You'd never do that."

But he hadn't believed her. She saw that in his eyes, heard it in his voice, felt it in the tension she could always feel in him when he was holding himself away from pain.

Now the image of another man swam before her eyes. He seemed vaguely familiar. She ought to know him, but didn't. Tall. Not as tall as Edward, but tall. And stocky. Threateningly strong. *Mr. Carlton's changed his mind, ma'am. He's given me a check for you, for any inconvenience. I'm to take you wherever you want, but you're to be gone before he returns.*

No!

"*No!*"

Jennie's cry hung in the darkness around her. She heard a door open somewhere in the house and hurried footsteps in the hallway. She wanted to recall her cry but knew that was impossible; she wanted to call out that she was all right, to escape from the inevitable loving inquisition, but she supposed that was impossible, too.

Her door opened. "Jennie?"

"Matilda? What are you doing here this time of night?"

The woman crossed the room with incredible silence. Jennie felt her sit beside her on the window seat and place her hand on Jennie's cheek, tracing her fingers across the tears that had escaped, unnoticed. "Dr. Freede thought it might be a good idea for me to stay close to you tonight."

Slowly, carefully, the woman turned Jennie toward her, running her hand in comforting circles over Jennie's back, feeling the tremors that shook her, tremors that only now Jennie noticed.

"Tell me, love. Tell me what happened."

"I don't know." She felt herself drawn, softly and tenderly, but with an undeniable strength, into Matilda's arms, into the loving protection—so different from Edward's— that now seemed essential to her very soul. "I don't know."

* 4 *

Edward couldn't believe it was nearly dark before he began to get free from the pressures of the day. He'd snatched a moment from the chaos early that morning to telephone Jennie, but Mrs. Winthrop had told him she was in the garden. He'd been disappointed but not alarmed then, nor in the afternoon when he'd received the same report when he'd called again. Jennie spent a lot of time in the garden. He knew that. He'd found her there more than once.

And all hell had broken loose in his offices in Houston, in San Francisco and even in Chicago at a time when his phone and fax lines were in transition.

Almost dark. He'd taken a few minutes for himself and gone into the room that once would have been perfect for Jennie's studio. Alone and quiet for the first time in hours, he looked into the shadows of the twilight and thought about Jennie's perpetual darkness. When he looked up, he found Lambert studying him from the hallway.

"Can we talk?"

Something in the sheriff's voice told Edward this was no question. That there could be only one answer.

"Come in and close the door."

Lambert nodded, stepped into the room and slid the heavy pocket door in place across the opening.

Realizing how dark the room had become, Edward pulled the chain on a nearby floor lamp and illuminated the corner where he stood. "What's wrong?"

"Jennie has remembered something."

From the expression on the sheriff's face, Edward knew it had not been a pleasant memory. "I'll go over right away. How is she?" He started across the room, only to find Lambert blocking his path.

"Shaken. Frightened, I think, but she won't admit to it."

Why was he standing there? Why didn't he step out of the way?

"Lambert—" Edward forced back his anxiety. Obviously, Lambert had something to say and wouldn't leave until he had said it. But now Edward wasn't sure he wanted to hear it. *God, Jennie,* he thought, *why didn't you call for me? Why didn't I know before this stranger?* "She remembers what happened?"

"Not completely. Only a portion. A small portion."

How small? Edward wondered. Not so small that it hadn't brought a hard lawman's edge to Lambert's usually soft voice.

"What?"

Lambert glanced at the grouping of chairs near the lamp and gestured toward them. After a moment's hesitation, Edward nodded. They sat together in silence while Lambert appeared to gather his thoughts. He reached once for his notebook and pen but left them in his suit pocket.

When he looked up at Edward, his expression reminded Edward of the first day they had met. All traces of softness gone, he looked suspicious and cynical.

"Jennie described a man, about five-ten to six feet, muscular, maybe two hundred pounds, with dark blond hair, brown eyes, a hairline scar on his forehead. He came to the apartment shortly after you left that day. He told her he had a check from you to pay her off and orders to take her anywhere she wanted so long as she was gone before you returned."

"God."

Edward was now grateful Lambert had insisted on sitting. He leaned back in the chair and closed his eyes, envisioning the scene. Jennie, shattered by the way he had so thoughtlessly initiated her in what should have been a gentle, considerate introduction to loving. Alone. God, he had left her alone in an apartment that he'd taken her to visit only a few times—far from enough times for her to feel at home there.

"And she went?"

At Lambert's continued silence, Edward looked over to see the sheriff studying him with a glacial expression in his eyes. "She's your wife," he said in a voice as cold as his eyes. "You've known her longer than I have. What do you think?"

The image of Jennie, alone and vulnerable gave way to one of her holding him. Here. In this house. *I love you, Edward. I always have. I always will. If I never know anything else about my life before Avalon, I know that.*

"No." He swallowed convulsively as he brought himself back to the reality of this interrogation, for that's what he now recognized it to be. "Of course she didn't go. Not willingly."

"And you, Mr. Carlton? Did you send someone to pay off your brand-new wife and get her out of your life?"

"*What?*"

"Or is Jennie's mind twisting the memory of another discussion? One with you, perhaps?"

Nothing and no one could have kept Edward in his chair. Restlessly, he paced across the room and returned to stare down at the sheriff. "Get this straight once and for all, Lambert. I loved my wife then. I love her now. I never have and never will intentionally hurt her."

As though unfazed by Edward's unleashed anger, Lambert merely stared back at him. "I find it remarkable," he said easily, "that while describing a man different from you in physical structure, Jennie also described a hairline scar on his forehead. While yours isn't quite where I would describe the forehead area, I suppose the similarity is too close to overlook. I hate coincidences, Carlton."

Edward scrubbed his hand over his eyes, trying to scrub away the images that hammered at him. One finally emerged from the morass and floated to the surface.

"The guard," he said as a sudden remembrance hit him. He continued, "Jennie had asked me about my scar. I'd gotten it on the *Lady B* when I was no more than eight or nine, but thought I knew enough about sailing to be the captain. I'd never noticed the security guard's scar before, but she did, the first time I brought her to the apartment.''

''You didn't mention the scar when you gave me his description.''

''I forgot!'' Edward stuffed his fists into the pockets of his slacks and turned away from Lambert, lowering his voice. ''I forgot. My God. Something as important as this, and I forgot.''

He heard the chair scrape against the tile floor as Lambert stood. ''Why don't you go on over to the vicarage, Edward. I'll tell your crew where you've gone.''

''Where are you going?''

Madeline caught the door of the Jeep just as Edward started to close it.

Edward looked at her blankly for a moment before realizing he had just walked from the house without telling anyone where he was going. ''To Jennie,'' he said.

''Now?''

He thought she paled, but in the shadowy twilight he couldn't be sure.

''The company is in turmoil and you're just walking away from it to go to a woman who has never known the meaning of the words *responsibility* or *commitment?* To a woman who has never wanted anything from you but the material things you could give her?''

''Madeline—'' He felt his anger rising at her, at her complete lack of understanding for Jennie. At her inability even to try to understand her.

''Edward, the Chicago office is supposed to call back at any moment. So is Gibbons.''

''You can handle it Madeline. Or Tim can,'' he said wearily. ''If not, it will just have to wait. My God, what time is it in Chicago, anyway?''

Her hand clenched on the car door before she released it and reached for his arm. "Edward, please—please—don't jeopardize all you've worked so hard for because suddenly this woman wants you again. Please stay."

"She's remembering." He took her hand and moved it, silently indicating he would close the door. Reluctantly, she stepped back. "I have to go."

Her mouth opened once, but she didn't voice the protest he saw forming. She was still standing at the edge of the driveway when he reached the line of fir trees and glanced back. He'd thought she understood him. Didn't she know that there was more in life than work, than business? He shook his head once, as though just waking from sleep. Once, he hadn't known there was. Once, he hadn't known Jennie.

Eleven

Reverend Winthrop opened the door.

"Where's Jennie?"

Winthrop stepped back to let Edward into the foyer. "You just heard?"

"Yes. My, God, yes. Otherwise I would have been here immediately. Where is she? *How* is she?"

"She's fine now, I think," the minister told him. "Still shaken, but basically all right."

"Has she remembered more?"

Winthrop shook his head. "No. At least not as of a couple of hours ago."

"Where is she?" Edward repeated and watched as a curious smile lighted the older man's face.

"She asked Jamie to bring a movie over. I'm afraid there's something of a sorority meeting going on at the moment, Edward, including all the women, and only the women, of the household."

* * *

Edward had never seen a television set in the vicarage. If he'd thought about it, he probably would have decided there wasn't anything so worldly or contemporary in the house. But there was one, along with a videocassette recorder, in the small but homey living room of the Winthrops' housekeeper, Caitlin.

And that was where the women were gathered. Jennie was sitting cross-legged on a floral love seat. Jamie was sitting beside her, holding a huge bowl of popcorn. Mrs. Winthrop and Matilda Higgins and Caitlin had drawn chairs close so that they could see the thirteen-inch screen where the movie *Casablanca* held them all enthralled.

The airplane had just lifted off, leaving tough-guy Bogey, playing tough-guy Rick, standing on the edge of the runway with Claude Rains, playing the French inspector. As they turned and walked away together, the theme music, which throughout the film had been the hauntingly beautiful "As Time Goes By," segued into the French national anthem and rose to fill the room.

Tears ran unchecked down Jennie's cheeks.

And Jamie's. And even Mrs. Higgins's.

"Oh, dear," Matilda said. "Can this be good for us?"

"Of course," Mrs. Winthrop told her after a moment of suspicious silence. "It's therapeutic." Glancing up, she saw Edward in the doorway and their gazes locked for a second. "But now, I do believe I'm hungry," she said. "Ladies, shall we move this meeting to the kitchen?"

Jamie looked up, too, and saw him. She set the popcorn bowl on the side table and clicked the remote control, silencing the TV as she rose from the love seat. "Good idea," she said. "No, you stay here," she told Jennie, who had started to rise. "You have company."

Edward stepped to one side as the women left the room, then he walked to Jennie. He knelt in front of her and placed a tissue from the box on the table in her hand. "You always were a softy for a sad film," he said.

"Edward?" She took the tissue, sniffed once and exhaled shakily. "So you told me. I guess some things don't change."

"This brought nothing back?" he asked, knowing she had to have been searching for more memories.

She shook her head. "This? No. Nothing."

What were they doing? They'd passed the time for polite conversation long ago, hadn't they?

"Why didn't you call me, Jennie?" he asked, wanting to take her in his arms, wanting to shield her from the pain of remembering and from the isolation of not. "Why didn't you let me know so that I could be with you?"

She didn't reach for him, and she didn't answer.

"My God, you don't think there was anything to that man's accusation? That I would ever do something like that to you—"

She dropped the tissue into her lap and caught his face in her hands. "No." She drew in a watery breath and pulled her hands away from him, picking up the tissue and scrubbing at her eyes. "No...."

But did she? There was something she wasn't saying.

"Jennie—"

"I was so scared," she whispered.

He took the tissue from her and dried her face then caught her hands in his. "Did you remember more?" he asked, not sure he wanted to know.

She shook her head, bit at her bottom lip, then thrust her chin out. Ah, Jennie. His brave, valiant Jennie.

"I was afraid you didn't want me any more. No one ever wanted me, Edward, did they? No one in my whole life wanted me."

Her words echoed a pain in his own heart, a pain that had only begun to ease since she had come into his life. "Or me," he told her, "until you. I want you, Jennie. I have since the day we met. I'll never stop wanting you."

Her voice shook with the intensity of her words. "Make love to me, Edward. Make me—God, I never thought I'd hear myself saying this. Make me forget."

He wanted to. Oh, how he wanted to. He released her hands and drew her to him, folding her in his arms, feeling the tremors that shook her slender body. She captured his face with her hands, and then she captured his mouth with hers. He tasted passion in her kiss, but he tasted the fear and desperation, too, and that was enough to remind him where they were.

"I want to," he murmured against her throat. "You can't know how much I want to."

"Then do it," she insisted. "Now. Please."

"Jennie." He brushed his lips across hers once, twice, then eased away from her, holding her away from him before he forgot all the reasons he must. "Jennie, we're in Caitlin's quarters, in the vicarage."

"Then take me home with you."

"I can't."

He felt the panic slowly draining from her, felt a reserve he was unaccustomed to seeing in Jennie. "I promised the sheriff I'd keep you here," he told her. "Where you'd be safe."

"Safe."

She pulled away from his touch, drawing back. He let her go. And when she began to rise from her place on the love seat, he rose, too, and stepped back so that she could. Not as graceful in this room, perhaps not as familiar with it as with others in the house, nevertheless, she paced restlessly.

"Then take me outside," she said finally. "I feel—I feel *caged* here."

He shook his head. "Jennie, it's late. It's pitch black in the garden by now."

She raised her head and met his gaze steadily. A tiny, bittersweet smile flitted across her face. "Then for a change, I'll guide you."

*   *   *

The garden wasn't quite pitch-black. Soft lights scattered along the paths cast faint illumination at their feet, and a full moon lined the leaves above them in silver. Between, the garden was filled with strange dark shapes and shadows.

Jennie moved confidently but restlessly along the path. Caged. Yes. That was a good term to describe the emotion her actions expressed.

And a good term to express how Edward was beginning to feel.

She moved past the bench where she had been seated the day he arrived. Avoiding the raised place in the path that had tripped her that day, she moved past the bench where he had found her with Jamie and the cat.

And although a gentle breeze stirred the night air, although distant birdcalls created soft music, Jennie seemed unaware of them.

She moved with a purpose he was afraid to interrupt, a concentration he knew better than to break, until she reached a small fountain near a stone wall and stopped. A huge tree draped branches over the fountain and over the wall, but the lower branches were bare. As Jennie leaned back against the trunk of that tree, the moonlight caught her in its glow, revealing the anguish she could no longer hide.

He remembered another fountain with Jennie standing beside it, with him watching her, wanting her then as much as he wanted her now.

I wanted you more than anything or anyone I had ever wanted, more than my next breath, more than my life if you weren't in it.

She'd said that. And he'd believed her. Or had he only wanted to believe her?

Make love to me, Edward. Make me—God, I never thought I'd hear myself saying this. Make me forget.

Was that what she had been doing yesterday? Forgetting? Forgetting how alone she must be in her world of darkness? *But you're not alone, Jennie. I'm here. I'll be with you if only you'll let me be.*

He'd wanted to believe her. Had she only *wanted* to believe him?

Damn. It had seemed so real. So right. But then, everything between them had always seemed real and right.

"Edward." She held her hand out toward him and he had no choice but to take it. He moved from the shadows to where she stood so clearly illuminated by the moonlight.

The touch of her hand in his was as potent as it had been the day before. As potent as it had always been. And as innocent.

He wanted her. Wanted her with an intensity that had him trembling with the need to take her.

She wanted—what? The knowledge that she wasn't alone? The comfort of another human being beside her in her darkness? A surcease from fear?

"I'm sorry, Jennie," he said hoarsely. "I can't begin to tell you how sorry I am."

She looked up at him and again he saw that tiny, bittersweet smile. "For what? For not wanting me as much as I want you? For not loving me? That seems to be the story of my life, doesn't it?"

Stunned, his hand tightened on hers until she gave a small moan. He dropped her hand. "You're out of your mind if you think that," he told her. "My God, Jennie, I wanted you so much, I convinced myself you were ready for us to go on together. I wanted you so much I—I, who should be protecting you—took advantage of your need and your fear and your loneliness—"

"And my love?" she asked.

He wanted to turn away from her but couldn't. Bracing his hands on the tree at each side of her face, he looked down into her eyes. "Yes."

She shook her head. "Oh, Edward, what are we doing to each other? I couldn't convince you before, either, could I? What do I have to do? You've brought me color and joy and life, here, and I know you must have in the months we knew each other before. What more could I have asked for? What more could I have wanted from you?"

She lifted her hand to his cheek. "You say you love me, but do you, Edward? Can you, if you don't believe I return that love?"

"Jennie—" No longer able to resist the sweet temptation that was his wife, Edward lowered his hands and drew her toward him. "Sweet, sweet Jennie."

With only the swift, almost silent rush of wind and a dull thud, something struck the tree scant inches from Jennie's head as he drew her to him. Bits of bark spat up from the tree.

For a moment, incomprehension held him motionless, and then he pulled Jennie against him and down onto the ground and into the darkness at the base of the tree as another shower of bark and splinters erupted from the tree.

"What—"

"Ssh," he said, placing his hand over her mouth. He waited, with only the sound of Jennie's breath near his ear and his blood roaring through his temples for what seemed an eternity. Finally, not entirely convinced they were alone but knowing they couldn't continue to stay there, he moved his hand from Jennie's mouth.

He spoke urgently in little more than a whisper. "There is light along the paths. I'm going to try to get us back to the house through the trees, without our being seen."

She twisted under the weight of his body, and a stray moonbeam reached the ground where they lay.

"Damn," he muttered, rolling with her into the shadows.

"Edward," she asked, whispering, too. "What's happened? What's wrong?"

He'd have given anything not to tell her, but to leave her in ignorance was to subject her to even more danger. "We have to get Lambert over here, Jennie. Now. Because someone just took a shot at us."

Sheriff Lambert was not happy. That knowledge finally penetrated the fog of panic that had wrapped itself around Jennie. Now, surrounded by the Winthrops, Matilda, Caitlin and Jamie, all the people she had grown to love, safe in the warmth and comfort of the Winthrop home and held in a possessive, secure embrace in Edward's arms, she allowed herself to think of the attack.

A shot. My God, someone had shot at them. Someone hated her enough to kill her.

Yes, she'd heard the story of how she'd been brought to Avalon, how she'd been left sightless and without memory. But because she had no memory of that, it had never seemed quite real. Perhaps a mistake had been made. Perhaps it was random violence, not truly directed at her. Perhaps there had been no true violence—that somehow, some way, she had managed to bring herself to New Mexico.

Now it was real.

Sheriff Lambert had arrived only minutes after they'd telephoned. He'd had them show him where the attack had taken place and had found not one, as Edward had led her to believe, but two bullets in the tree where she had been standing. He'd spoken of calibers and velocity and tangents. What she'd understood was that someone with a high-powered rifle had taken position, probably somewhere in the cemetery behind the church next door, and had waited to fire until she and Edward were outlined in the moonlight. What she understood was that if Edward had not taken her in his arms when he did, she, and possibly he, too, would be dead right now.

The sheriff stopped speaking into the telephone. Jennie heard the soft click of the receiver being replaced as Edward tightened his arm around her.

"A neighbor on the next street called to report a strange pickup truck with a camper shell and an out-of-state tag parked in the alley. By the time our officer responded to the call, someone had jumped in the truck and driven off at a high rate of speed. We have the tag number and a description of the vehicle."

"But not of the person," Edward said.

"Male. Maybe six feet. Stocky."

Jennie felt a chill shudder through her. The man was tall. Not as tall as Edward, but tall. And stocky. Threateningly strong. *Mr. Carlton's changed his mind, ma'am. He's given me a check for you, for any inconvenience. I'm to take you wherever you want, but you're to be gone before he returns.*

"The man in my memory?" she asked.

"May be, Miss Jennie. May be. We got word of a man fitting his description trying to sell some of your paintings in Santa Fe yesterday. He got away, but the gallery owner is holding your paintings for us."

"And has he been in the area all this time, or has he decided to make a return visit, for some reason?"

Jennie heard the anger and frustration in Edward's voice, but Lambert answered only the spoken question. "We don't know. If he's been here, he's been well hidden."

"Jennie's supposed to be safe here. That was why I let you talk me out of fighting to take her away. That was why I left her here with Reverend and Mrs. Winthrop—"

"Mr. Carlton," the sheriff said in what Jennie now recognized as his official voice, "you might want to consider that while Jennie has been the victim, you have been the true target of the events of the past few months."

She felt the taut muscles of Edward's chest convulse as Lucas's words struck, but he didn't release her. "I'm taking my wife home with me tonight, Lambert. Don't try to stop me."

"And expose her to even more danger?"

"How? I have a higher wall, a locked gate, a security alarm—"

"And more people coming and going than some retail stores, as well as a household staff you don't know—"

"A household staff provided by your very own, well-recommended Marianna Richards, who has had free run of this house for the past six months—"

"Stop it! Both of you!"

Jennie pulled herself out of Edward's arms and stepped between the two men. "Did either one of you think about asking me what I want to do?"

At the silence that surrounded them, she had her answer. No. Of course not.

It was Edward who broke the tense silence. "What do you want, Jennie?"

He didn't know. That much was evident from his hesitation. But he was willing to give her a choice. That much was evident, too. When would he realize that where he was concerned, she had no choice?

She held her hand out to him. "I want to be with you."

Edward held Jennie while she slept. He'd almost lost her—again. Another second and a stranger's bullet would have stolen Jennie's life from her. And from him.

The breeze came through the open windows of his bedroom as it had the last time he'd lain here with his wife, and the moonlight danced across her face, lighting then shadowing the woman who had become more precious to him than his own life.

The gate was locked. The alarms were secured. All the windows on the lower floor were closed and locked. The sheriff's deputies regularly drove past the estate grounds, and downstairs Tully Wilbanks, Matilda Higgins's nephew and Lucas Lambert's first deputy, kept guard in the house.

All his corporate staff had returned to the lodge, except for Madeline, whom they had earlier decided would temporarily take quarters in the house to remain close to the still-fractious telephone and electronic communications center. She hadn't been happy to see Jennie, hadn't been happy to learn that danger had possibly followed them home. But she'd refused to leave, refused to remove herself from that danger, saying that he'd need her help the following morning.

Another one of her headaches had attacked Jennie after they arrived at his house. He'd given her some of the heavy medication Matilda had sent with them. Now she sighed, as though the pain had finally eased, and turned in his arms, burrowing close to him in her sleep.

Jennie.

She said she loved him; she'd told him that over and over. Why had he never really believed her? What was there in him that had made believing so impossible that it took an assassin's bullet to make him see clearly what he should have known from the beginning. Jennie never lied. That was one of the things that had first drawn him to her. So why had he forgotten that? But he had, until she had stretched out her hand to him, knowing he might be taking her into even more danger, and said *I want to be with you.*

I want to be with you, too, Jennie, he promised as he brushed his lips over her short, tousled curls. But now Lambert's words returned to haunt him. Was it possible that he was the target? That what had happened to Jennie wouldn't have happened if he hadn't been in her life?

He couldn't believe it. If that were so, whoever was responsible would be demanding something from him in return for her safety, not just taking her away from him. That was the way it worked. He, of all persons, ought to know.

No. Lambert was missing something. Slater was missing something. *He* was missing something. This had to be coming from Jennie's past. Otherwise, he'd never be able to forgive himself for all she had suffered, all she had lost, because of him.

The residue of her headache lingered until late the following afternoon, leaving Jennie feeling dull and thickheaded. Edward had hovered over her almost all day, leaving only when a grim Madeline Harrison had summoned him for one emergency or another.

They'd stayed at the vicarage the night before only long enough for Matilda to pack a small overnight case for her. She'd wanted to come with them, but, mindful of possible danger, Jennie had insisted she not.

Before breakfast, however, Marianna Richards had arrived with a garment bag and suitcase and had helped Jennie dress.

And that afternoon, Matilda's nephew Tully had returned and relieved the deputy who had been on duty during the day and brought word that his aunt was coming the next morning, regardless of Jennie's objections.

Except for the animosity she felt coming from Edward's assistant, which, for the most part, Madeline disguised as no more than a cool, polite and formal facade, Jennie felt she might still be living in the warmth and familiarity of the vicarage.

Business as usual, she thought as once again Edward sought her out to touch her face, to ask how she felt, to treat her as though she were infinitely fragile, and once again Madeline summoned him to a telephone call.

And once again she began to feel caged.

She needed to be outside. The vicarage garden had always been her salvation. She'd spent hours there fighting the terror of not knowing who she was or why she was, of being afraid, so very afraid no one would come for her. Now that solace had been taken from her. Oh, it was a fair exchange, and one she had made willingly. Edward for a garden. There was no comparison.

But still . . .

There was a garden here. Not one that she knew well. But a portion of it. Yes, she knew that. A fountain. A place where they had picnicked. A place where she had dared tell Edward how much she wanted him.

A place where she dared go now, if for only a few minutes, to finish clearing the fog from her brain.

What danger could there be? The outer streets were patrolled regularly. Tully was here in the house. Edward was only a raised voice away.

From the increasing darkness of her shadows when she reached the fish pond, Jennie knew that night was rapidly approaching. But the air was so fresh here, so fragrant with spring flowers and the pervading aroma of distant pine. The leaves rustled above her head in the slight breeze, and the fountain bubbled merrily.

Minutes passed before she became aware of footsteps behind her. Edward, stealing another few minutes from what had to have been a hectic day to check on her again.

She turned with a welcoming smile for him. "It's almost as wonderful here today as it was—"

A hand clamped across her mouth. An arm yanked her against an unfamiliar body. A man's voice grated in her ear. "Be quiet if you know what's good for you."

Good for her? *Good for her?* her mind screamed as panic began descending on her. But she couldn't afford panic. She had to think—had to escape.

She had been turning when the hand covered her mouth and as it moved now to capture her more completely, she twisted again, sinking her teeth into something fleshy and soft. She heard a grunt from the voice in her ear, felt a brief relaxation of the arm that held her. Clawing, biting, kicking, she fought her way free of the man who held her, screaming once for Edward before she silently scrambled into the nearby shrubbery, feeling the branches clawing at her skirt, at her skin. She suppressed a shudder. Better the branches than the unknown man. The night was growing dark; she'd already noticed that. Was it dark enough to hide her?

"Jennie!"

She heard Edward's harsh cry from the house. Too far. He was too far away. And then shouts, running footsteps, a groan and the sound of flesh striking flesh. Oh, God. What was happening?

"He got away! Catch him, Tully," Edward yelled. "Jennie! Jennie, where are you?"

She wanted to stay hidden forever; she wanted to throw herself in Edward's arms and scream out her fear. She did neither. She stood, quietly, outwardly calm, inwardly shaking. "I'm here."

She didn't have to throw herself into Edward's arms. He grabbed her shoulders, looking at her, she knew, examining her for injuries, then with a groan he hauled her against him. "No," he said quietly, viciously, over and over, and it was like an oath or a mantra. "No, no, no. Not again. No one is ever going to take you away from me again."

From somewhere far away, she heard the roar of an engine, then closer, another one, and the scream of sirens as tires spun on the driveway. Edward released her only enough to turn her so they could start back to the house.

Madeline met them at the side door. "What in God's name is going on? Edward? Edward, are you all right? Your shirt is torn. My God, what happened to your face?"

"You're hurt?" Jennie asked, coming out of the blessed numbness that had overtaken her when Edward wrapped her in his arms.

"It's nothing. Madeline, call Lambert. Have him get some more men over here."

"Let me take care of that cut first—"

"Now!"

Twelve

Within minutes, Lambert arrived, bringing with him two deputies who immediately fanned out and began searching the grounds. The sheriff exchanged one long, silent glance with him as Edward opened the door for him. Just as silently, Edward led him to the room in the center of the house where Jennie was waiting. Once there, Lambert nodded at Madeline but walked directly to the wing chair where Jennie sat, looking small, vulnerable, and defenseless.

"Are you all right, Jennie?" Lambert asked, kneeling in front of her and reaching out to trace a scratch on the back of her hand. "Did he hurt you?"

"No." She looked up in what had to be an instinctive gesture, searching the room. "He only frightened me. Edward?"

"I'm here, Jennie," he told her as he walked to her side and placed his hand on her shoulder. He felt her sigh and then shudder before she lifted her scratched hand to cover his.

Lambert glanced at their two clasped hands then rose to his feet. "Tully is still in pursuit," he said. "Along with a couple of state troopers. He said the gate was open when he left. Does anyone know how that happened?"

Edward whirled to look at Madeline. Everyone had been aware of the need for increased security. How in hell had the gate been left open? She shrugged, showing her concern and her own questions. "Tim left...not long ago," she offered hesitantly. "Perhaps—perhaps he didn't completely secure it behind him."

Lambert turned on Edward. "You're passing out keys?"

"No," Madeline assured him. "We've been opening the gate electronically from the control panel here in the house."

"And after the attack, you just decided to leave it open? My men and I weren't stopped by the gate or by a staff member. Anyone could have come up that driveway."

Madeline raised her head regally. "Yes, Sheriff, I suppose you're right. But then, the only person we have to worry about is well away from here by now, somewhere in the mountains, I presume, so why shouldn't we have left the gate open for you?"

A deputy arrived at the door, holding a cellular phone in his hand. "Sheriff, Tully wants to speak to you."

Lambert took the phone and walked to the other side of the room. "Yes, Tully. What have you got?"

He listened for a moment and when he turned back to the room, his eyes narrowed.

"We have his truck."

Edward felt Jennie's shoulder tense beneath his hand.

"You and I need to take a look at the truck together, Carlton. Tully found some paintings in it. And a few items that seem to match the list you gave me of things taken from your apartment."

Edward saw the moment Jennie realized that the man who had grabbed her only minutes before had to be the same person who had robbed her of her sight and her memory.

She stood abruptly, still holding his hand. "I'll go with you," she said. "I don't want anything happening to you. I—I don't want to be separated from you again."

"No," Edward said, hearing Lambert's voice echoing his.

"No," Edward repeated. And he didn't want to be separated from her. Somehow, this moment seemed more fraught with danger than any that had gone before. But he knew he had to think of her, not himself. "You're too vulnerable. Stay here. Wait for me where I know you'll be safe."

"Actually, I'd rather you wait at the vicarage, Miss Jennie," Lambert said. "After what has happened here tonight, I'm not so sure this house is a good place for you to be."

Edward wanted to argue, but once again he had to admit the sheriff was right. He nodded abruptly, in agreement.

"And what about me?" Madeline asked. "Are you leaving me alone in this mausoleum with a madman on the loose?"

Lambert shook his head. "As you said, Ms. Harrison, he's probably well away from here by now, somewhere in the mountains. And there's never been any attempt to harm you. I believe you'll be safe here. With the pursuit, I don't have anyone I can leave with you, but I do have men on patrol in Avalon, and they will be only a telephone call away."

"Lock the gate after us, Madeline," Edward said, knowing the truth of the sheriff's words but still reluctant to leave her alone. "And lock the house. We'll be back as soon as possible, but if you'd feel more secure with company, call the lodge and ask Tim and the crew to return."

* * *

Alerted by a telephone call from the sheriff, Matilda Higgins met them at the vicarage.

"Where are the Reverend and Mrs. Winthrop?" Edward asked.

She smiled ruefully. "A wedding rehearsal. The Johnson girl, Sheriff, you know her, and Will Hanson's boy. They'd left long before you called, but they should be back any minute now."

Lambert nodded. "It will have to do. Lock yourself in, Matilda, and don't leave Jennie alone for a minute."

Matilda placed a comforting arm over Jennie's shoulder. "I'll take care of her. I promise you."

Edward took Jennie's hands in his. He wanted to do more, to hold her close, to chase the shadows from her eyes, but he sensed Lambert's growing impatience to get on with whatever this evening held.

"Be safe," she whispered.

"I will. And so will you. I'll be back soon. This is almost over, Jennie. It has to be."

Once back in the Land Rover, Edward waited for Lambert to say something. He didn't, simply headed in the direction of his office.

"You've towed the truck in?" Edward asked.

Lambert nodded. "And your former security guard."

"What? You've caught him? Then what was this charade all about?"

"An abundance of caution," Lambert told him, and Edward had no idea what he was talking about. "I hope."

Jennie refused to go upstairs to the room that had been hers for the past six months, choosing to wait instead in the comfortable front parlor. Her tension was almost gone, soothed away by the blackberry tea Matilda brewed for her and the easy companionship of the woman who had become her friend. Only fear for Edward's safety kept it from sliding away into the mist swirling around her.

Fear. And the return of her headache. Which descended upon her in full violence and without warning only moments after Edward left her in Matilda's keeping.

"Are you sure you won't go upstairs, love? Only for a little nap? Your Edward will be all right, and you need to lie down and let your medication work."

But just as Jennie refused the nap, she also refused the heavy medication, insisting on something milder that would ease the pain at least a little but not send her into a never-never land.

"He'll be back soon, Matilda," she insisted. "He promised. And I want to be waiting for him when he returns."

But when the doorbell rang stridently, insistently, less than an hour later, it wasn't Edward who Matilda admitted into the house, but Madeline who entered the parlor sounding distraught and far from the cool, poised and slightly cynical woman Jennie had known her to be.

"Lucas's office just called," Madeline said without preamble. "Something's happened. They want me to bring you to headquarters right away."

Jennie rose from her chair, feeling a wave of dizziness strike her. "Edward?" she asked. But she knew the answer. Nothing else but harm to Edward would have affected Madeline this way.

"I don't know," Madeline said. "The caller wouldn't say."

"Oh, my Lord." Matilda placed her hand on Jennie's arm, steadying her. "I'll get my purse. We'll go right away."

"No." Now Madeline hesitated. "Mrs. Higgins? I—the—Tully Wilbanks is your nephew?" she asked, sounding almost abrupt. Matilda must have nodded or made some sign. "I'm sorry. He's been injured. The caller said you were to go directly to the hospital."

Jennie hugged her nurse, feeling the woman's shock and concern. "Go," she said. "I'll be all right with Madeline for the few minutes it takes to get to the sheriff's office."

Matilda returned her hug, tightly. "Thank you. I'm so sorry, Jennie."

Jennie nodded and released her. "I know. We all are. Madeline?"

"Yes," the woman said, taking Jennie's arm in her hand and half leading, half pulling her from the room. "Let's hurry."

At the sidewalk, both women fumbled while Madeline opened the door and seemed almost to be pushing Jennie into the car.

"Wait," Jennie said. "I can do this. Just—please—step back," she asked as she seated herself and swung her legs into the vehicle.

Madeline slammed the door shut. A moment later, the driver's door opened.

"Edward's Jeep?" Jennie asked as she felt Madeline tug the seat belt around her and lock it into place.

"Yes." Madeline started the engine. Jennie heard the click of the automatic door locks as the vehicle lurched out into the street. "It was parked behind my rental. It was faster to bring it than to move the cars."

Faster, but not really Madeline's style at all. She must really be rattled, Jennie thought as she felt the uneven brick roadway beneath the wheels of the speeding vehicle. Soon the bricks gave way to the conventional paving on the outskirts of town. Minutes passed.

Too many minutes, Jennie realized as she surfaced from her worry about Edward's safety.

They should have reached the sheriff's office in a matter of moments.

And now the roadbed changed again.

"Madeline?" she said.

The woman's silence was her only answer.

"Madeline?" Jennie repeated. "Where are you taking me?"

"Madeline."

Edward was numb from the revelations the security guard had just made.

"Madeline. I can't believe it."

Lambert rested a hand on his shoulder. "I'm going to go pick her up now. Do you want to be there?"

"That's why you moved Jennie. You suspected. God. That was why you didn't want me to take her to the house with me, wasn't it? You suspected Madeline even then?"

"I hoped I was wrong, Carlton. I still wish I had been. Are you coming with me?"

"Yes." Madeline. My God. He'd trusted her as he had never trusted another person in his life. He'd trusted her more than—*more than he had trusted Jennie.* "Yes. I want to see her face. I want to hear her tell me—tell me *why.*"

The gate was open when they reached the estate. His Jeep was missing from its parking place. The front door was unlocked. The house was empty.

A chill settled over Edward when he realized Madeline was no longer there. Lambert snatched up a telephone. "Get someone over to the Winthrop house," he ordered. "Now!"

They were on their way to Jennie when the call came over Lambert's radio. Matilda Higgins was at the hospital, asking about Tully.

The street in front of the vicarage was alive with blue lights and marked and unmarked cars when they arrived, but they were all too late. Jennie was gone.

Lambert had a description of the Jeep broadcast within moments of their arrival, but how much of a head start did Madeline have? Long enough for Matilda to have gotten to the hospital, to determine that Tully wasn't there and to contact the sheriff's office.

Long enough to—God, no. Madeline wouldn't harm Jennie. She couldn't. He'd trusted her. Valued her friendship. Believed that she'd felt the same.

"We have state and county people looking for the Jeep," Lambert told him, breaking into his reverie. "And for the two women. I don't believe Ms. Harrison can get out of the county—"

"Out of the *county?*" Edward asked. "With or without Jennie? You suspected this, Sheriff. Where was the protection that should have been in place? Why wasn't there someone watching Madeline? How did this happen? Why in God's name didn't you take Jennie with us or leave me with my wife?"

Lambert was silent for a moment, accepting Edward's accusations. "I don't believe Ms. Harrison can get out of the county," he repeated. "I'm not sure she'll try. At least not for a while. You know her better than any of us. Do you have any idea where she might go?"

"Know her?" Edward felt those words slide bitterly from his throat. "I didn't know her at all."

"Think, Carlton. Think! Tell me anything about her that will help me find her."

Before it's too late. Those words hung unsaid between them.

Edward pulled into himself, thinking.

"She's precise," he said. "Restrained. Cool." He laughed bitterly. "And obviously insane."

"Not insane," Lambert said. "Driven, perhaps. But this whole plot denies it was conceived in insanity. Go on," he urged. "What else?"

Edward closed his eyes, picturing Madeline, efficient, dependable Madeline in her office, with that wide expanse of polished desk gleaming between them. "She believes everything must be taken in order, and finished in order, with every punctuation mark and completed form in place.

And she has an almost compulsive belief that everything must balance—from spreadsheet accounts to plants on a shelf."

Now Lambert seemed lost in thought. Finally, though, he snapped to attention. "Come on," he told Edward. "I think I know where she's gone."

"Where?" Edward asked, reaching for the car door as he spoke.

"Where else? Where it should have ended once before."

She couldn't get the seat belt unfastened. Something seemed to be wedged in the mechanism. Jennie twisted and yanked on the fastener as Madeline sped along the highway.

"And what will you do if you get it undone?" Madeline snapped. "Jump out of a speeding car? That might make it easier for me, after all."

No. She wouldn't jump out of the car. She *couldn't* jump out of the car. Each time she managed to get the door unlocked, Madeline slapped the automatic lock back on.

"Why are you doing this?" Jennie asked. "Edward trusted you. Don't you know what your betrayal will do to him?"

"Whose betrayal, Jennie? Yours is the only one he's going to know about. I'll be just an innocent victim. How sad that I was duped into going after you, that the two of us were kidnapped by—what is his name? I don't think I ever heard it. But you know it, of course. The security guard at Edward's apartment? Your lover. The two of you had worked this long before the wedding. In fact, there wouldn't have been a wedding if you hadn't—what? Had a fight with your lover? Found out you were pregnant?

"Yes. I like that," Madeline said with satisfaction, before continuing.

"And you—lost the baby? Had an abortion?—and then, of course, after you found that you could marry Carlton money, your lover returned and the two of you hatched the plot to steal what you could from Edward. What happened, Jennie? Did your lover become jealous? Was that why he tried to kill you? Yes. I think that's probably it. I think that's probably what I heard while I was struggling for my life.

"And I'll be injured. Regrettable but necessary. I do hope it doesn't take them too long to find me, handcuffed as I will be to the steering wheel of this—this truck.

"Edward will be so sorry that I've suffered the way I have—that I even attempted to save your miserable life—that maybe, without too much delay, we can get back to where we were before you disrupted his life and mine. Now, where the hell is that road?"

Jennie renewed her efforts to release the seat belt as the Jeep bounced over a rutted-out roadbed and slewed into a sharp turn.

"And just where *were* you, Madeline?" Jennie asked, praying for time, praying for the strength to escape from this woman. "Before I disrupted your life?"

Madeline gave a small yelp of pain as the Jeep left the roadway and bounced back down.

"He's mine, Jennie. We're too much alike not to be together. I've known it for years. Then you came along and in a matter of weeks all my work was destroyed. He can't see me as anything other than an extension of the office."

"He trusted you, he believed in you. And he rewarded you well for your work."

"Now he'll marry me. Now I'll truly be a Carlton."

"My God. You'll destroy him. He told me about his family. He can't go through this again. And you can't get away with it."

"Of course I can. I thought this out very carefully. Edward will never believe that anything other than something in *your* past brought this on. He can't let himself. Otherwise, yes, the guilt would destroy him. But he's spent twenty-five years distancing himself from that pain. Why do you think it was so easy for him to accept you'd left him? *He won't let it touch him again.* And that is exactly why I will get away with anything I do and with anything I tell him."

Jennie shrank back against the seat. Edward wouldn't believe her. He had proof that at least a portion of Madeline's story was made up of lies. But that wouldn't do Jennie any good. If Madeline had her way, she'd be long dead before he ever heard the lies.

The Jeep braked to an abrupt halt, throwing Jennie against the restraint of her seat belt. Madeline muttered something under her breath and slammed the car in reverse, backing up with a shower of small stones and the squeal of protesting wheels, then spun it to the left.

Jennie's head pounded, and her heart felt as though it were going to beat its way out of her chest, but she couldn't give in to either pain or fear. *Think!* she ordered herself. And even though she didn't know what good it would do, she sensed she had to keep Madeline talking, keep her mind occupied, keep her distracted.

"Are we lost, Madeline?"

"Shut up, will you? Just shut up. It's around here somewhere. I know it is. It just doesn't look the same at night as it did when I drove out here and found it."

Found what? her mind screamed, but Jennie forced her voice to remain soft, almost inaudible so that Madeline had to work to hear her. "Found what?"

"The place you're going to die, Allison Jennifer Long," Madeline said with what sounded like true satisfaction. "The place you *would* have died six months ago had that incompetent piece of trash I hired done his job correctly. At least he's done something right," she added, almost conspiratorially. "He's escaped, so there won't be any problem putting the blame for this on him, too."

"Hurry," Edward said again. "God, man, can't you get any more speed out of this thing?"

No lights or sirens marked their pace as Lambert's Land Rover and a following deputy's cruiser sped across country, churning over back roads, ditches and open stretches of mountainside as they headed for a spot Edward had never wanted to see again.

"Not if we want to get there alive," Lambert said grimly, fighting the wheel.

"How much longer?"

"Soon," Lambert said. "Soon."

As the Land Rover slewed around a curve, its headlights swept across a tableau Edward knew he would never forget. His Jeep sat at an angle blocking the excuse for a road, with both doors open. And at the edge of the mountainside, Madeline was struggling with Jennie. An inert Jennie.

For a moment, as the headlights caught her in their glare, it almost appeared that Madeline was pulling Jennie back from the precipice.

Lambert slammed on the brakes and both men jumped out of the car, running.

"Edward!" Madeline screamed. "Help me!" She released her grip on Jennie—dead? Please, God, no. Unconscious?—and threw herself at him. "Thank God you're here. Down there, Sheriff." She pulled herself away only far enough to gesture toward the narrow path that led down to the overhang where Jennie had been found so many months before. "He ran that way when he heard you coming."

Her betrayal twisted at his heart. Still he wanted to believe her innocent. Wanted to believe he hadn't been so misguided in his trust. "Who, Madeline? Who ran away?"

"The security guard from your building, Edward. I recognized him even before they started talking. He was waiting in the car when I picked up Jennie after the call from the sheriff's office. He was her lover—"

He stiffened and pulled away from her, keeping his hands tight on her shoulders. "Lambert."

"Right."

Lucas stepped to his side and took Madeline's arm. "Ms. Harrison," he said as the following squad car spun onto the roadway and skidded to a stop, "you have the right to remain silent..."

Edward dropped to his knees beside Jennie. She was breathing. That much he could tell. He traced his fingertips over a gash near her temple. He forced himself not to gather her close, not to risk injuring her any further than she was already injured. *What had Madeline done to her?*

"Jennie," he whispered brokenly. "Jennie, I'm so sorry. Please wake up. Please be all right. Jennie, you've got to forgive me for this. I can't live with myself if you don't."

Almost as though she heard him, she moaned. Slowly, much too slowly for his peace of mind, she opened her eyes.

"Jennie?" Her name was little more than a whispered prayer.

She reached for his hand, and he grasped hers, holding tight. She returned the pressure of his fingers with a light pressure of her own and smiled—a small, tender, healing smile. "You came."

Jennie lost consciousness again before they reached the hospital and did not regain it through the trauma-room examination or treatment, nor when placed in a private room in an exclusive wing of the new hospital.

Edward insisted on accompanying her to that room. Lambert insisted on accompanying him.

And through the night, as he waited, holding his wife's hand, Edward slowly became aware of the repeated sweep of headlights across the window, of the restrained noises coming from the parking lot.

Reluctantly, he released Jennie's hand and went to the window to look out. The parking lot was full of cars, of almost silent people. Waiting. Waiting for what?

"It looks as though half the town is out there," Edward said as Lambert joined him at the window.

"More than that," Lambert told him.

"Why?"

Lambert looked back at the unconscious woman. "She's theirs," he told Edward. "They adopted her months ago. Haven't you seen how much the people in this town love Jennie?"

"No one ever wanted me," Edward repeated.

"What?"

"That's something she said to me not long ago."

"Well, Avalon wants her," Lambert told him. "Just look at the people waiting for word of her condition, if you have any doubts."

"And I want her," Edward said softly.

"I know," Lambert told him. "I know."

Even without opening her eyes, Jennie knew she was back in the hospital. The sounds and scents were too familiar to mistake. Her head pounded, and as she twisted her head on the pillow, she felt the slide of a bandage against the pillow.

Madeline?

What had happened to Madeline?

And what had happened to her?

She heard the small moan that escaped her and then felt a hand clasp hers.

Edward.

He was with her.

Of course he was with her. Hadn't she known he would be? Hadn't she known he wouldn't believe Madeline's lies?

Hadn't she known he would never—ever—betray her love by trying to send her away?

She remembered.

All of it. God, no wonder she hadn't been able to remember before.

This time, she didn't try to suppress her moan.

"Jennie?"

His voice was harsh, strained. His hand tightened on hers.

"Jennie, love. It's over. You're safe."

"And you?" She couldn't open her eyes yet; she couldn't face the darkness. "Are you all right?"

"Yes."

"I'm glad."

"How can you be?" Harsh. Strained. Full of pain. "After what happened, why don't you hate me?"

"Hate you? Edward—" She had to do this. For him, if not for herself. Had to stare once more into those vaporous gray scarves. Had to open her eyes for Edward and convince him that nothing and no one could ever make her hate him.

The room was a pale gray, swirling with shadow. Early morning? Possibly. In the structured environment of the hospital, who could tell? But something was different. Something was subtly, infinitesimally different.

Almost afraid to breathe, Jennie realized what it was. One by one, slowly, inexorably, those gray scarves clouding her vision were being pulled away.

Two men stood beside her bed. One, as tall as Edward, had to be Lucas Lambert. He'd carried her too often for her not to recognize him. And Edward.

Leaning over her, his face taut with worry.

She moistened suddenly dry lips. How unkind the past months had been to him, giving his face new lines, lines that were only partially visible to her but enough so that she knew they were there.

She could see!

Not well. Not clearly. But she could see.

Wondering, she lifted her hands to Edward's face in a gesture that had once been as natural to her as breathing.

"Edward?" she whispered.

He closed his eyes briefly in relief, but not before she saw a glint of moisture. Relief that she lived; that she reached out for him.

He didn't know yet that she remembered or that by some miracle she might again have sight. She'd tell him. Soon. But for now, she'd relish another miracle—that of being here. With him. With a glorious future—together—spread out before them.

"Welcome back, my love," he said, at last bending and drawing her into his arms, where she belonged. "Welcome home."

*   *   *   *   *

SILHOUETTE®
Desire
CELEBRATION 1000

A treasured piece of romance could be yours!

During April, May and June as part of Desire's Celebration 1000 you can enter to win an original piece of art used on an actual Desire cover!

Or you could win one of 300 autographed Man of the Month books!

See Official Sweepstakes Rules for more details.

SILHOUETTE DESIRE® "CELEBRATION 1000" SWEEPSTAKES
OFFICIAL RULES—NO PURCHASE NECESSARY

To enter, complete an Official Entry Form or a 3"x5" card by hand printing "Silhouette Desire Celebration 1000 Sweepstakes," your name and address, and mail it to: In the U.S.: Silhouette Desire Celebration 1000 Sweepstakes, P.O. Box 9069, Buffalo, NY 14269-9069, or in Canada: Silhouette Desire Celebration 1000 Sweepstakes, P.O. Box 637, Fort Erie, Ontario L2A 5X3. Limit one entry per envelope. Entries must be sent via first-class mail and be received no later than 6/30/96. No liability is assumed for lost, late or misdirected mail.

Prizes: Grand Prize—an original painting (approximate value $1500 U.S.);300 Runner-up Prizes—an autographed Silhouette Desire® Book (approximate value $3.50 U.S./$3.99 CAN. each). Winners will be selected in a random drawing (to be conducted no later than 9/30/96) from among all eligible entries received by D.L. Blair, Inc., an independent judging organization whose decision is final.

Sweepstakes offer is open only to residents of the U.S. (except Puerto Rico) and Canada who are 18 years of age or older, except employees and immediate family members of Harlequin Enterprises Ltd., their affiliates, subsidiaries, and all agencies, entities and persons connected with the use, marketing or conduct of this sweepstakes. All federal, state, provincial, municipal and local laws apply. Offer void where prohibited by law. Taxes and/or duties are the sole responsibility of the winners. Any litigation within the province of Quebec respecting the conduct and awarding of prizes may be submitted to the Regie des alcools des courses et des jeux. All prizes will be awarded; winners will be notified by mail. No substitution for prizes is permitted. Odds of winning are dependent upon the number of eligible entries received.

Grand Prize winner must sign and return an Affidavit of Eligibility within 30 days of notification. In the event of noncompliance within this time period, prize may be awarded to an alternate winner. Any prize or prize notification returned as undeliverable may result in the awarding of that prize to an alternate winner. By acceptance of their prize, winners consent to the use of their names, photographs or likenesses for purposes of advertising, trade and promotion on behalf of Harlequin Enterprises Ltd., without further compensation unless prohibited by law. In order to win a prize, residents of Canada will be required to correctly answer a time-limited arithmetical skill-testing question administered by mail.

For a list of winners (available after October 31, 1996) send a separate self-addressed stamped envelope to: Silhouette Desire Celebration 1000 Sweepstakes Winners, P.O. Box 4200, Blair, NE 68009-4200.

SWEEPR

As seen on TV!
Free Gift Offer

With a Free Gift proof-of-purchase from any Silhouette® book,
you can receive a beautiful cubic zirconia pendant.

This gorgeous marquise-shaped stone is a genuine cubic
zirconia—accented by an 18" gold tone necklace.

(Approximate retail value $19.95)

Send for yours today...
compliments of ▼ *Silhouette*®
™

To receive your free gift, a cubic zirconia pendant, send us one original proof-of-purchase, photocopies not accepted, from the back of any Silhouette Romance™, Silhouette Desire®, Silhouette Special Edition®, Silhouette Intimate Moments® or Silhouette Shadows™ title available in February, March or April at your favorite retail outlet, together with the Free Gift Certificate, plus a check or money order for $1.75 U.S./$2.25 CAN. (do not send cash) to cover postage and handling, payable to Silhouette Free Gift Offer. We will send you the specified gift. Allow 6 to 8 weeks for delivery. Offer good until April 30, 1996 or while quantities last. Offer valid in the U.S. and Canada only.

Free Gift Certificate

Name: _____

Address: _____

City: _____ State/Province: _____ Zip/Postal Code: _____

Mail this certificate, one proof-of-purchase and a check or money order for postage and handling to: SILHOUETTE FREE GIFT OFFER 1996. In the U.S.: 3010 Walden Avenue, P.O. Box 9057, Buffalo NY 14269-9057. In Canada: P.O. Box 622, Fort Erie,

---

FREE GIFT OFFER   079-KBZ-R
ONE PROOF-OF-PURCHASE
To collect your fabulous FREE GIFT, a cubic zirconia pendant, you must include this
original proof-of-purchase for each gift with the properly completed Free Gift Certificate.

079-KBZ-R

MILLION DOLLAR SWEEPSTAKES
AND EXTRA BONUS PRIZE DRAWING

You're About to Become a *Privileged Woman*

Reap the rewards of fabulous free gifts and benefits with proofs-of-purchase from Silhouette and Harlequin books

Pages & Privileges™

It's our way of thanking you for buying our books at your favorite retail stores.

Pages & Privileges™

Harlequin and Silhouette— the most privileged readers in the world!

For more information about Harlequin and Silhouette's PAGES & PRIVILEGES program call the Pages & Privileges Benefits Desk: 1-503-794-2499

Silhouette®

SD-PP123